# Disney Learning

## Wonderful World of

# ANIMALS

# Wonderful World of Animals

## Parent's Note

*Are dogs really related to wolves? How do snakes crawl? What is the biggest animal?*

*Disney's Wonderful World of Animals has been created to answer these and so many other questions that will allow your child to learn about animals in a fun and meaningful way. Formatted in a simple question-and-answer style, this book has been designed to appeal to a child's limitless curiosity about the fascinating world of animals.*

*Simply organized, each chapter profiles animals with questions accompanied by lively answers written by animal experts. Stunning full-color photographs and favorite Disney characters accompany amazing facts and fascinations and help to make the real-life learning come to life.*

*Disney's Wonderful World of Animals has been designed as a learning tool that is certain to educate children while inspiring a lifelong respect for the amazing creatures with which we share our planet.*

For information address Disney Press,
114 Fifth Avenue, New York, New York 10011-5690.
Visit www.disneybooks.com

Printed in Singapore
ISBN: 0-7868-4961-4
Library of Congress Cataloging-in-Publication Data on file

First Edition
1 2 3 4 5 6 7 8 9 10

Written by Donald E. Moore III, PhD.
Vetted by Scott Silver, PhD., Patricia (Trish) Cole, PhD.,
Bill Holmstrom, Paul Sieswerda, Mark Halvorsen
Designed by Editions Play Bac, Paris, France
Special thanks to the experts at Disney's Animal Kingdom Theme Park
at Walt Disney World Resort.
Disney character art © Disney Enterprises, Inc.
Pixar character art © Disney Enterprises, Inc./ Pixar Animation Studios
All rights reserved.

# Table of Contents

# Our Fascination with Animals

Wildlife is all around us—sometimes in the most unexpected places! Learning about the amazing array of animals around us and how they live is important to understanding our environment. From the tiny mice and spiders that are often hidden from view to the most unusual creatures swimming in the sea, you'll discover all sorts of fun and strange facts! What's the fastest animal? Which one is the most dangerous? You'll find answers to these questions and more in your travels through the wonderful world of animals.

## What is an animal?

Animals are complex living things. They exist all over the world in every habitat you can imagine, from lush rainforests to frozen tundras, from deserts to the depths of the ocean. Some animals fly, some swim, some make noises, while others communicate solely through body language. Some live in family groups while others grow up without ever seeing their parents. Yet this amazingly diverse group is all related on some level and *you* are a part of it!

## We're animals, too!

People are a kind of animal called mammals. Mammals, which also include animals such as cows, dogs, and monkeys, often have hair, and they suckle their young with milk. Worms, insects, fish, frogs, snakes, and birds are animals, too. Animals can be helpful to us, or harmful. And, there are many animals that are still a mystery to us.

▲ Mammal    ▲ Bird    ▲ Amphibian    ▲ Insect

## How do scientists identify animals?

Just as you might organize similar books on the same shelves, scientists who study living things organize or classify them into scientific categories. The animal kingdom consists of mammals, birds, fish, insects, reptiles, and amphibians—plus a few other types of creatures. Some of these animals, called vertebrates, have backbones. These can be anything from giraffes and owls to eels and toads. Other animals in the world are without backbones; they are the invertebrates. Worms, snails, and spiders are all invertebrates. Organizing similar animals according to classifications helps scientists understand how different kinds, or species, of animals are related to one another and how they all fit into the natural world.

▲ People love to spend time with animals, whether as pets, in zoos, or even in the wild.

▼ Many animals take care of their babies just like human mothers do.

Each large grouping of animals can be further sorted into smaller groups. Although each species of animal might be known by anywhere from one to a dozen common names, it has only one scientific name. The mountain lion, for example, may be called a puma, catamount, panther, and many other names, but its unique scientific name is "Felis concolor."

Scientists classify animals according to six different scientific groups. These six categories are: kingdom, phylum, class, order, family, genus, and species. Imagine the mountain lion. This animal belongs to the animal kingdom, right? It also has a backbone, and so it fits into the phylum called Chordata, which is made up of vertebrates. It belongs to the class of mammals, known as Mammalia. It is

## Animals through History

We know that animals were important to people even in ancient times. Can you imagine being a human hunter back in the Stone Age? You probably would have tried to find animals by listening to the sounds they made, following the tracks they left behind, or sniffing around for their unique scents. If you were the only cave dweller looking for animals (either to eat the things they were eating, or to eat them!), you wouldn't need to tell others where they lived. But cavemen lived in family groups and developed ways of commu-nicating with others about where food was available. For example, they might have led other cavemen to the animals or shown other cavemen how to find them. Ancient people also eventually developed cave and rock art showing different animals!

As early as 15,000 B.C., humans showed their fascination with animals through cave paintings.

also a meat-eater, and so it is part of the order called Carnivora. The mountain lion is a type of cat; the cat family is referred to as Felidae. Finally, the mountain lion's scientific name, as you know, is Felis concolor. "Felis" is the name of the animal's genus, and "concolor," which means "of one color," is its species. This form of classification can be used to sort all kinds of living things.

We, too, can be classified by scientists! How might you fit into the animal kingdom? Like the mountain lion, humans are members of the phylum Chordata and the class of Mammalia. We are part of the order of Primates and the family of Hominidae. The scientific name for a human is Homo sapiens, which means "wise man."

There are more than 350,000 beetle species in the world with even more to be discovered!

## Are there animals still waiting to be discovered?

Although it might seem like we know everything there is to know about the natural world, we don't know everything yet! As you read this book scientists are still exploring, and there are many discoveries to be made. These discoveries will help us understand how we affect the world and how animals and their habitats can benefit us. Some of our classifications of animals might change in the future with new discoveries and new scientific information.

## Are farm animals and pets related to wild animals?

Over the course of many generations, humans have gone from hunting animals—like our cave-dwelling ancestors did—to raising animals for such products as milk, eggs, wool, and even companionship. Our ancestors spent many years learning how to develop the breeds of domestic animals we have today. The cows, chickens, sheep, and dogs we have on our farms or in our homes all have wild ancestors from centuries ago. These animals provide us with the food, clothing, and protection that help us survive wherever we live in the world.

## Are some animals in danger of extinction?

Yes. More humans live on Earth today than ever before. Because people are taking up more space on the planet, some of the animals in the world are disappearing. And animals that become extinct disappear forever.

People use the habitats of animals as places to live, and cut down forests for wood or to make more space for houses. Our search for gas and oil, which we use for fuel and heat, as well as our use of pesticides when we grow crops, can pollute animal habitats. We need to protect animals—and the habitats in which they live—from the danger of extinction.

## Making discoveries

Like our ancestors, we are still fascinated by wild animals. Many people go on whale watches, visit aquariums, or take vacations to Africa, the Amazon, or the Arctic to observe animals in nature. However, the creatures in our backyards, local parks, and zoos are just as fascinating as the wildlife living in far-off places. If you want to discover animals, you just have to remember to look for them! It may be as simple as looking out your window to see birds feeding nearby. Listen for animals wherever you go. If your parents or teachers say it's safe to feel the scales, feathers, or fur of an animal, go ahead and touch it! Your journey into the wonderful world of animals can start with this book. Just turn the pages to learn more about the amazing animals around you!

 From 20,000 feet in the sky to more than 25,000 feet below the sea, animals inhabit every part of our world.

▲ Leopard

# Mammals

A mammal is a **vertebrate** that has hair and feeds milk to its young. Most mammals give birth to live young, although there are a few mammals that actually lay eggs. Did you know that humans are mammals? Thanks to our unique hair and our fat layers, we mammals have better control over our body temperature than creatures like reptiles and amphibians; we're known as **warm-blooded** animals. If necessary, we mammals can shiver to warm up when we are cold; many mammals also can sweat to help keep cool when it's hot outside.

▲ Virginia opossum    ▲ Brown bears    ▲ Coyote    ▲ Chimpanzees    ▲ African elephant

Because mammals can control their body temperature, they are adapted to live in many extreme environments—from the cold polar regions to the hot tropics, and from the dry deserts to the wet rainforests.

Many kinds of mammals roam the Earth and even the sea. Kangaroos and koalas, dogs and horses, cows and rabbits, hippos and mice are all mammals. Whales and dolphins, which might look like big fish, are warm-blooded and nurse their young with milk. They are mammals like us.

Mammals also come in an amazing array of sizes, from the tiny flying bumblebee bat, which weighs about as much as four small coins, to the ocean-dwelling blue whale—known as the largest animal ever to have lived, at more than 135 tons (that's heavier than a loaded airplane!). Mammals live in all kinds of places, too. Some mammals, such as naked mole rats, spend their entire lives underground. Others, like sloths, hang out in trees every day.

And think about how unusual mammals can be! There's the armadillo, with a body covered in armor, and don't forget the funny-looking platypus, a mammal designed to live in the water. With its webbed feet, bill, and flat, furry tail, it's hard to imagine that this critter could be related to us!

*Humpback whale* ▶

# Monkeys & apes

Monkeys and apes have two unique characteristics among animals—hands that can grab and eyes that face straight ahead. Foward-facing eyes allow them to see precise distances as they jump and grab at branches, which is useful for animals that hang around in trees! These mammals live in all kinds of habitats, including forests, grasslands, and even deserts.

*Rafiki know you should look straight ahead—toward the future!*

## Do monkeys really swing with their tails?

Some South American monkeys have grasping, or **prehensile**, tails. Prehensile tails act like a fifth hand. They help monkeys move safely and quickly through the jungle. These creatures can even hang upside-down using their tails, leaving their hands free to grab branches and pieces of food.

▼ *Chimpanzees use a stick to capture termites.*

## Are monkeys and apes smart?

Monkeys and apes have some of the biggest brains of any mammal. And, some people think animals that use **tools** are smarter. An animal might make a tool to help make it easier to do a job—like catching food. Chimpanzees (members of the ape family) often strip the leaves from a stick and use it to capture termites. They push the stick into a termite mound, pull it back out, then lick all the termites off the stick. Pretty smart, don't you think?

**Smallest primate:** Mouse lemur of Madagascar, less than 2 ounces

**Largest primate:** Gorilla of Africa, more than 600 pounds (4,800 times larger than the mouse lemur)

**Species of primates:** About 230

▲ *Japanese snow macaques warm up in a hot spring.*

## Do monkeys "talk" to each other?

Scientists think that monkeys and apes communicate very well. Behavioral researchers have discovered that African vervet monkeys alert comrades with different alarm calls when danger nears. They make one noise at the approach of eagles, which hunt from the air, and another sound at the sight of leopards, which hunt from the ground.

## Do any primates live where it snows?

Monkeys and apes have developed behaviors that let them live almost anywhere—from the semi-desert areas of Africa to the cold mountains of Asia. Hamadryas baboons have thin coats which keep them cool as they forage for food in dry African gorges, while Japanese macaques live in the snowy regions of Japan and have thick coats of hair to keep them warm.

## Do monkeys and apes have families?

Sure they do! Gibbons and gorillas have families, while other monkeys, such as baboons, live in larger groups called "troops." Monkeys and apes behave a lot like people. For example, tamarin monkeys from South America baby-sit their siblings, so that they will know how to take care of their own babies when they grow up to have their own families.

# Rodents

About half of all mammal species are rodents! There are 1,700 different kinds, including squirrels, mice, and porcupines. Rodents include jumpers like jerboas, swimmers like muskrats, and diggers like prairie dogs and groundhogs. They can have bushy tails, naked tails, or armored tails. The most bizarre rodent may be the naked mole rat, with its tiny eyes, naked body, and projecting incisor teeth.

## Is it true that rodent teeth grow all the time?

Yes! Wouldn't it be strange if your teeth never stopped growing? Rodent front teeth, called "incisors," grow throughout the creature's life. The outer surface of a rodent's tooth is harder than the inner one, so each tooth becomes sharper—like a chisel—every time the creature chews. If you have a pet rodent, such as a guinea pig or hamster, make sure your pet has something like wood to chew to keep its teeth healthy.

## Why do beavers build dams?

Beavers build impressive dams using cut trees and mud. Damming a stream creates deep, quiet ponds where water surrounds and protects the beavers' lodge. Dams are built higher than the water level and may be repaired and extended over the years by generations of beavers. Dams are usually about 65 feet long, but can be almost 2,000 feet long! Lodges are roomy inside and may have an internal chamber about six feet around.

## Are rabbits rodents?

No. Ground-dwelling rabbits, hares, and pikas might look like rodents, but these creatures are in a separate mammal group.

Rabbits have two pairs of upper **incisors**, while rodents have only one pair. Rabbits and hares also have long ears that help them shed extra heat and hear predators approaching.

◄ A beaver carries a branch back to the lodge.

**Smallest rodent:** Pygmy mouse of Central America, only 1 inch long and 7 grams (about 20 small coins)

**Largest rodent:** Capybara of South America, weight over 170 pounds

**Most social rodent:** Naked mole rat, Africa; naked mole rats live in underground colonies of up to 100 or more individuals.

## How do rodents protect themselves?

Some rodents, like spiny mice and porcupines, have special sharp hairs called "**quills**" that help protect them from danger. Each porcupine has tens of thousands of quills, making them some of the best-armored mammals ever. Porcupines don't purposely shoot quills off their bodies; the quills are so lightly attached to the porcupine's body that they immediately adhere to any predator that touches them. Ouch!

North American porcupines have thousands of quills.

Mice eat berries and other nutritious fruit.

### Why do we need rodents?

Rodents are nature's collectors. Chipmunks stuff food into their jaw pouches to store underground. They may store fruits and seeds in several different burrows. Burrowing helps turn soils and allows water to flow to deep plant roots.

Rodents are also nature's foresters. Gray squirrels and other squirrels are important to the life of the forest. They bury a lot of their food in the summer and fall, but often don't find it again. Those lost nuts and seeds become many of the new trees and shrubs that sprout each year!

Rodents also are nature's builders. Beavers build dams, lodges, and canals. Colonies of mole rats excavate complex tunnel systems. Muskrats and other aquatic rodents make grass lodges in swampy areas. Squirrels create tree cavities and leaf nests. The ponds behind beaver dams provide feeding, resting, and nesting sites for migratory birds.

# Elephants

I may be the biggest animal in the jungle, but the lion is king!

Elephants are another type of amazing mammal. These giants are known for their big ears and long trunk. There are three kinds of elephants—Asian elephants, which live mostly in grasslands; African elephants, which live on the savannah; and African forest elephants, which live in the jungle. Asian elephants are among the smartest animals and they're helpful, too! People have used them to help with tasks such as logging for hundreds of years.

Not just a nose! Elephants use their trunks as hands to pick up small objects.

## How do elephants use their trunks?

The elephant's trunk is an extension of its nose, but also can be used as a hand. An elephant can lift its trunk high up in the air to smell something far away. Elephants also use their trunk for close-up smelling and touching, and for grasping food and bringing it to the mouth. Mother elephants also can use their trunks to pick up a baby elephant. The end of an elephant's trunk is very flexible and can be used like a finger; with this "finger," an elephant can pick up something as small as a coin!

## How can you tell whether an elephant is African or Asian?

Asian elephants have smaller ears than African elephants. African elephants' heads are shaped like a dome, and their trunks have two fingerlike tips at the end. Asian elephants have two dome shapes on the top of their head and just one "finger" on their trunk.

Asian elephants have two domes on their heads.

**Largest African elephant:** Weight up to 8 tons (16,000 pounds) and can stand 13 feet at the shoulder

**Largest Asian elephant:** Weight to 11,000 pounds, shoulder height 8–9 feet

**Elephant calf at birth:** Weight over 200 pounds, 3 feet tall

**Closest living relative:** Hyrax

**Number of toenails, African elephant hind foot:** 3

**Number of toenails, Asian elephant hind foot:** 4

**Digestion time, elephants:** 60 hours

**Digestion time, humans:** 24 hours

**Number of muscles in an elephant's trunk:** 40,000!

Adult African elephants are very large, powerful animals.

## Why do elephants have such huge ears?

Here's where elephants' big ears come in handy—they can hear their neighbors "talk," even from several miles away! Elephants can talk to one another using "infrasound," a sound that is so low humans cannot hear it. If you were ever close enough to elephants that were talking, you would be able to feel the vibration the way you can sometimes feel the rumble of thunder.

Elephants also use their big ears to cool down. That's why you might see them flapping their ears when it's hot outside.

## Do elephants really have good memories?

Most definitely! Elephants live long lives, so a good memory is very helpful. For example, they can remember friends from neighboring herds and recognize members of their extended family. When they face a drought, the older elephants remember where to find a good water supply and can lead the rest of the herd there. Elephants that have been looked after by humans even remember their caretakers after years of separation.

# Hoofed animals & their relatives

Ahh, that's more like it. I needed to take a load off my hooves!

Pigs, hippos, camels, deer, giraffes, antelope, and their cousins all have a horny hoof on each toe, which is used for gripping the ground, and long, flat teeth for chewing plant leaves. Some hoofed animals also have long legs for running. A few others, such as camels, cows, deer, and their relatives, have special stomachs so they can swallow their food, then go elsewhere to chew and digest it when no predators are around.

## Why do camels have humps?

Humps might look funny, but they are very useful. Did you know that camels can survive for days without food or water? These mammals live in desert areas where food is often in short supply. When food is plentiful, the camel's body turns that food into fat and stores it in its hump. Then, when food is scarce, camels use the fat in their humps. Special body chemistry turns each pound of fat into energy and water. Camels with one hump are called "**dromedaries**" (a "D" turned sideways looks like one hump), and two-humped camels are "**bactrians**" (a "B" turned sideways looks like two humps).

▼ Bactrian camels have two humps.

▲ The two-toed soft foot of a camel helps it walk on sand.

**Tallest living animal:** Giraffe, Africa. Record height more than 19 feet

**Heaviest hoofed mammal:** Hippopotamus, Africa; about 10,000 pounds

**Fastest hoofed animals recorded:** Pronghorn, North America (52 mph); Thompson's gazelle, Africa (48 mph); Saiga, Russia (48 mph)

**Largest deer:** Moose, North America. 7–8 feet tall, over 1,800 pounds

**Smallest hoofed mammal:** Mouse deer, India and Asia. 2–12 pounds

*Male deer grow new antlers every year.*

## What's the difference between horns and antlers?

Cows, goats, sheep, and antelope have **horns**, which are bony and grow throughout the animal's life. We can tell the age of some of these animals by the number of rings that appear on their horns. **Antlers** fall off and regrow every year. Deer have antlers that grow every spring, then drop off every winter in a process called "shedding." In almost all deer species, only males grow antlers, but in reindeer and caribou, males and females grow antlers.

## Are pigs really smart?

Believe it or not, studies have shown that pigs are at least as smart as dogs. They have a great sense of smell and hearing, and they can communicate with family members by scent as well as grunts and other sounds. Trainers can teach pigs to fetch, to sit, and to do many of the other tricks that dogs can perform.

*Domestic pigs live in family groups.*

*Giraffes have special grasping lips to help them eat leaves from tall trees.*

## What are those pointy things on a giraffe's head?

Those pointy things are short horns covered with hair. They grow on top of giraffes' heads. Male or female giraffes can have one or two pairs of these horns. Some even have another small knob between the eyes!

# Bears

Black bears, brown bears, panda bears, and polar bears are the most famous of the world's eight kinds of bears. Bears can be kind of small (for bears!) and only weigh 100–200 pounds; or, they can be huge. Arctic brown bears and polar bears can stand ten feet tall and weigh between 1,000 and 2,000 pounds! Bears are mostly found in northern habitats.

Grrr! I can growl as well as any bear. Even better!

▲ Salmon is a great source of protein for brown bears.

## What do bears eat?

Bears have a well-balanced diet because they eat almost anything. Black bears and brown bears eat insect grubs or small rodents, as well as grass, nuts, berries, and other sweet things like honey. Polar bears eat mostly seals and fish found in the cold arctic. Sloth bears eat lots and lots of ants, which live in mounds in their tropical habitat. Pandas eat mostly bamboo, a common plant in the hills of China where they live. Each kind of bear knows just where to find the foods most common in their habitats, where their ancestors have lived for thousands of years.

## How big are bear cubs?

When they are born, the cubs, often twins, are blind and helpless and weigh less than one pound! Mother bears find a protected place, such as a rock den, a snow cave, or a hollow tree, to have their tiny babies.

**Largest living bear:** Polar bear, more than 1,700 pounds

**Largest extinct bear:** Giant short-faced bear of the Ice Age, over 2,000 pounds

**Smallest living bear:** Asian sun bear, about 60 pounds

**Longest swim by a bear:** Over 40 miles recorded for one radio-tagged female polar bear in one day, Norwegian Arctic, July 2005

**Polar bear milk fat content:** About 30 percent

**Dairy cow milk fat content:** About 4 percent

Polar bears are well adapted to live in the harsh Arctic environment.

## Do bears hibernate?

Many bears sleep through winter and when food is scarce. However, there are some scientists that do not think it's accurate to call bears hibernators. True hibernators, like chipmunks, actually become cold during their winter sleep; their heart rate slows down, and they cannot be awakened. Unlike chipmunks, bears, if disturbed, might wake up.

## Are polar bears all white?

Believe it or not, polar bears are black under all that fur. Their fur is actually transparent, but many of these hairs put together look white in daylight—just like snow! These hairs reflect sunlight differently throughout the day; at sunset, they might look light orange, and in lower light, they might look light blue.

## Are all bears dangerous?

They can be—they are **carnivores.** Most bears will avoid people and want to be left alone. But some bears attack—mother bears will defend cubs that you may not even see. It is best to make lots of noise in the woods to make sure not to startle mother bears.

Mother bears are powerful protectors of their cubs.

# Cats

Once the sun goes down, it's time to hunt!

Cats are carnivores that have short faces, big, pointed teeth, and sharp, curved nails to capture prey. All cats are expert hunters and they are very quiet when pursuing their prey. Most can pull their claws back into their paws when they do not need them so that they stay protected and sharp. Cats have hairy, not bushy, tails, and rough tongues that they use to clean their fur.

▼ Cheetahs can reach speeds of up to 70 miles per hour!

## What's the difference between a leopard and a cheetah?

Although both leopards and cheetahs have spots that help keep them hidden in forests or grasslands, they have different predatory jobs, or ecological niches. Leopards hide in the forest or grass to wait for prey, and their large, muscular legs and necks help them drag the prey into trees away from lions and hyenas. Cheetahs are more doglike—they are built almost like racing greyhounds. Their slender legs are built for speed and help them chase down antelope and other fast prey.

**Largest wild cat:** Siberian tiger, head to tail length more than 10 feet, weight more than 600 pounds

**Smallest wild cat:** Blackfooted cat, head to tail length about 2 feet, weight 3–6 pounds

**Highest elevation cats found:** Snow leopard, at more than 18,000 feet in the Himalayas

**Fun fact:** Only big cats roar. Only small cats purr.

A deer's worst nightmare, the eyes of a big cat searching for prey

## Can cats see color?

Cats have excellent vision so that they can capture quick-moving prey. Cats can see some color, but their color vision is not like ours because they are more nocturnal than humans. They can tell red from blue, but red and green look similar to them.

Most animals that are active in the daytime, especially colorful animals like parrots, shallow-water fish, and insects, can see lots of colors. Humans can see colors from deep red through dark violet and all the rainbow colors in-between. Other animals can see reds we cannot see ("infrared") and violets we cannot see ("ultraviolet").

## Can cats swim?

You might not think so, but yes! Tigers and jaguars will jump into water to catch their prey. Other cats also swim through streams, rivers, swamps, and lakes in their habitat. Although they might appear to dislike it, they do need to get around—and sometimes the fastest way to get somewhere is by swimming!

Bobcats keep their powerful claws clean with their rough tongues. ▶

# Marsupials

Kangaroos, koalas, North American and South American opossums, and other animals have pouches and are called **marsupials**. They give birth to tiny babies that are blind, bald, and helpless. Each baby crawls into its mother's pouch, where it spends many weeks, growing and developing before it emerges.

Parents will do anything to protect their children, Simba.

▲ A baby kangaroo is called a "joey."

## How many types of marsupials are there?

Scientists estimate there are more than 250 kinds. These include North America's only marsupial, the Virginia opossum, South America's mouse opossums, Tasmanian devils, and Australian bandicoots, wombats, and kangaroos.

## Why do kangaroos have tails?

Kangaroos, wallabies, and other large, hopping marsupials usually walk slowly, using their tail and front paws as a tripod support while their hind legs swing forward. When they are frightened, kangaroos stand tall on their powerful legs and race off in long hops, moving more than 30 miles per hour; they can even jump over fences ten feet high! When they move like this, they use their tails for balance and to turn quickly.

## What do you call a group of kangaroos?

A group of kangaroos is called a "mob." There are many different kinds of marsupials, but, unlike kangaroos, most do not live in groups.

My mother used to carry me around by my neck!

**Largest marsupial:** Red Kangaroo, more than 5 feet tall and almost 200 pounds

**Smallest marsupial:** Australia's 2-inch-long little pygmy possum

**Size of newborn marsupial:** Jelly bean-sized

**Best digger:** Wombat, Australia

**Best "flyer":** Sugar glider, Australia

**Best swimmer:** Water opossum, Central and South America

## Do kangaroos really box?

Not quite. Kangaroos have a large claw on one of the toes of each hind foot. When they defend themselves, they rear up on their strong tails and kick out. To kick more effectively, a kangaroo may try to wrestle close to its opponent, holding the opponent with its front legs—making it look like they're boxing.

## What do koalas eat?

Koalas are marsupials that live in eucalyptus trees. When they want to eat, they just reach out and grab a bunch of fresh leaves.

The Virginia opossum is the only North American marsupial. ▶

▼ Koalas live in Australian forests.

# Dogs, wolves & foxes

Wild dogs, such as wolves and foxes, look a lot like pet dogs. They have long snouts, powerful teeth and jaws, and clawed toes that help them grip the ground as they walk or run. They use their long, bushy tails to communicate which of them are leaders and which are followers. Leaders hold their tails high, while followers keep their tails under their bodies.

Man, it's tough to be a hyena with all these foxes around!

## What are foxes like?

Foxes are small or medium wild dogs that usually live alone. There are several kinds of foxes—including arctic, kit, gray, and red. They eat bugs, small birds, and small mammals, such as mice. Gray foxes can climb almost as well as cats and, like other foxes, often scurry into hiding before you see them.

*Red foxes are solitary animals.*

**Largest wild dog relative:** Gray wolf, northern hemisphere worldwide. Can weigh more than 175 pounds

**Heaviest domestic dog breed:** English mastiff 160–230 pounds, can be more than 300 pounds

**Tallest domestic dog breed:** Irish wolfhound, 35 inches at the shoulder (6 feet tall when standing on hind legs!)

**Smallest wild dog relative:** Fennec fox, North Africa; only 2–3 pounds

**Smallest domestic dog breed:** Chihuahua, Mexican; 2–6 pounds

## What do dogs and their relatives eat?

Almost all dogs and their relatives eat meat and some plants. Foxes and jackals also eat insects and fruit, as well as small rodents and rabbits. In general, larger dogs like wolves often eat beaver, antelope, or deer.

## Why do dogs sniff?

Studies have shown that dogs not only can hear sounds at least four times better than we can, but their sense of smell is at least 40 times better than ours. Wherever an animal goes, it leaves a certain scent. A dog's nose can detect those scents, which give the dog information about recent visitors.

## Can dogs talk?

Dogs communicate with one another using facial expressions, body language, scents, and noises. Domestic dogs howl like wolves when they are looking for group members, bark at danger, and make other noises when they play.

If it weren't for those wolves, we'd be runnin' the joint.

▲ Domestic dogs make great pets.

▲ Coyotes howl to communicate their location.

## Why do wolves travel in packs?

Working in a pack, wolves are able to capture larger prey than animals that hunt alone. Together, they can attack a large moose, while a wolf hunting alone would never be able catch something so big.

### How do guide dogs help people?

For almost 100 years, certain kinds of domestic dogs have been trained to assist people who are blind or deaf. These dogs can be trained to open doors, lead blind people across streets or up and down stairs, or alert people who are deaf when the phone rings.

27

# Whales & dolphins

Whales and dolphins are different from all other mammals because they have no fur, although they may have hairy bristles on their faces. A layer of fatty **blubber** keeps them warm in cold ocean waters. Their flattened tails, called "**flukes**," and large front flippers help these fish-shaped mammals to swim. But unlike fish, they have to go to the water's surface to breathe.

*It would appear that marine mammals use their flippers much the way I use my wings!*

## What is the world's biggest marine mammal?

The world's biggest animal is the blue whale, which can be 100 feet long—that's more than two school buses put together! Blue whales weigh more than 240,000 pounds, so they need to eat a lot of food. They dine exclusively on small crustaceans called krill, and can eat up to 40 million krill in one day!

## Are dolphins different from whales?

There are two kinds of whales. Some species such as humpback whales have mouths full of whalebone, or **baleen**, through which they strain plankton and other small animals. Other whales, such as sperm whales and orcas, are toothed whales. They use their teeth to catch and eat larger prey. Dolphins are considered small-toothed whales.

▼ *Dolphins are among the most intelligent mammals.*

## Are dolphins smart?

Dolphins are famous for their intelligence and for their ability to behave in complex ways while in the wild and in human care. They have a strong family life, are very social, and are even known to help their companions when they're in distress or danger.

## Do dolphins smile?

Dolphins have what looks like a smile, but that is just how their mouths are shaped.

**Deepest whale or dolphin dive:** Sperm whale, over 6,500 feet

**Longest whale or dolphin dive:** Sperm whale, about 1½ hours

**Largest dolphin:** Orca, 9 tons, swims almost 35 miles per hour

**Fun fact:** Sailors used to carve whale teeth into decorative objects called "scrimshaw."

*Humpback whales are easy to identify because of their long white flippers.*

## Do dolphins and whales get along?

They can, but normally they do not live together.

## Do whales and dolphins really sing?

Dolphins and whales use different sounds to communicate and find their way in the water, but most do not really sing. Male humpback whales are one of the exceptions—they sometimes sing long songs to stay in contact with other whales or to attract a new girlfriend!

# Wild! Mammal World-Record Holders

I'll be the best king and make my father proud!

Mammals come in all shapes and sizes. They roam the land and swim the seas. They can be champion divers, runners, hunters, builders—even champion sleepers! Here is just a sampling of some wild records held by mammals.

## WORLD'S FASTEST LAND MAMMAL

The cheetah can run at a speed of about 70 miles an hour. That's faster than a car on the freeway! What makes a cheetah want to run so quickly? It has to be very fast to catch its food: antelope. Cheetahs can only sprint for short distances, so the antelope are often able to escape.

## WORLD'S SLOWEST LAND MAMMAL

When it does move, the sloth only goes about one mile every four hours! The sloth lives in the tropical forest, where, for most of its life, it hangs out—literally!—upside down in trees. Because it eats the handy tree leaves and some fruit, it doesn't have to chase its food down as the cheetah does.

## WORLD'S FASTEST AQUATIC MAMMAL

The cheetah may be the fastest mammal on land, but the orca, or "killer whale" takes first place in the water. This aquatic mammal can swim up to 35 miles an hour!

## WORLD'S BIGGEST LAND MAMMAL

The African elephant can weigh up to eight tons (16,000 pounds), and stand thirteen feet tall at the shoulder—that's as heavy as a school bus and as tall as two basketball players stacked on top of each other! The biggest African elephant tusk ever recorded weighed 258 pounds!

## WORLD'S BIGGEST MAMMAL

The blue whale is the biggest creature ever to live on Earth. It weighs 150 tons and, at 100 feet long, it's longer than two school buses lined up one in front of the other. Can you imagine that? This giant ocean mammal is even bigger than the largest of the dinosaurs!

## WORLD'S SMALLEST MAMMAL

Weighing in at a mere two grams, adult bumblebee bats from Thailand are the world's smallest mammals. They get their name from their diminutive size, which is about that of a large bumblebee!

## WORLD'S BEST BREATH HOLDER

Sperm whales can stay underwater for more than one and a half hours! Their heartbeat slows down while they dive, and this helps them hold their breath for a long time.

## WORLD'S TALLEST MAMMAL

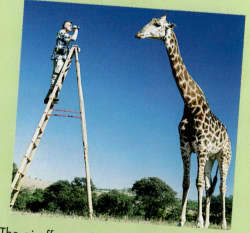

The giraffe stands head and neck above the rest. The world's tallest animal, it can stand over ten feet tall at the shoulder. From there to the top of the giraffe's head is another eight to nine feet, making the giraffe as tall as 19 feet! How many bones do you think are in a neck that long? A giraffe's neck has only seven bones—the same as in your neck!

## WORLD'S FASTEST-GROWING MAMMAL

Blue whales and fin whales have babies that are 20 feet long at birth. Those hefty newborns then start growing another two feet every month—that's almost one inch every day! How long does it take you to grow one inch?

▲ Alligator

# Amphibians & reptiles

All amphibians and reptiles are **cold-blooded** and most adult amphibians and reptiles have two pairs of legs for moving on land. However, amphibians and reptiles are different in some ways. Amphibian skin needs to breathe, so these creatures most often have moist, slimy skin that does not have scales. Reptiles breathe with lungs and have watertight skins covered with scales, so they can live successfully in drier habitats. Reptiles have claws on at least some of their toes, while most amphibians don't have any.

▲ Alpine newt      ▲ Rattlesnake      ▲ Strawberry dart poison frogs      ▲ Gila monster      ▲ Galápagos tortoise

Many amphibians live two lives in one! ("Amphi" means two or both, and "bio" means life.) Amphibians spend part of their lives in water and part of their lives on land. Since amphibian **eggs** are laid and develop in water, many adult amphibians need to live in or near water. Reptiles, on the other hand, lay eggs with watertight shells or give birth to live young, so they can survive farther away from water.

Reptiles include turtles and tortoises, snakes, lizards, and a "living fossil" called a "tuatara." Amphibians include frogs and toads, salamanders, and an unusual kind of legless amphibian called a "caecilian."

Spring is when most amphibians move to the water, where they visit breeding sites and mate. The females' eggs—which are laid and fertilized in the water—look like clear jelly with dark polka dots in the middle. From these eggs hatch young amphibians, called **"tadpoles"** or "pollywogs." They have gills like fish, and no legs. But later in life, they'll go through something called **"metamorphosis"** and change into adult amphibians.

Do you know that some of the most poisionous and venomous creatures on Earth are amphibians and reptiles? Luckily, they are usually easy to identify. From brilliantly colored poision dart frogs to hissing rattlesnakes, they clearly say, "Don't mess with me!"

*Cobra* ▶

# Frogs & toads

Frogs and toads are amphibians. Of the 4,000 amphibians jumping around out there, about nine out of ten are frogs or toads! Frogs have smooth, moist skin, while toads have drier skin covered with warts. All frogs and toads croak, chirp, or have singing calls. They make these noises using something called a vocal sac, which is in their throat area. Some species have two vocal sacs, one located near each ear.

I bet I can hop like a frog!

## Is a frog tadpole different from a salamander tadpole?

A tadpole is the early developmental stage of an amphibian. A frog tadpole has what looks like an enlarged "head" and a tail—the "head" will become the head and body of the adult frog. Salamanders are more fishlike in shape and keep their tails as adults. Frog tadpoles have tiny teeth for eating aquatic plant material. Salamander tadpoles have a wide mouth that gets even bigger as they grow. They eat insects and crustaceans, and sometimes each other.

## Why do toads have warts?

Those bumps that you see on a toad are not really warts, and they cannot give you warts. The bumps are skin glands. These glands, especially the ones near the toad's eyes and ears, produce repelling or poisonous substances that help protect them from predators. Animals that lick toads such as the ten-inch marine toad get very sick and can even be paralyzed by the poison! So be sure to always wash your hands very well after touching toads or other animals.

## What do frogs and toads eat?

When tadpoles hatch, they eat algae and some small, slow-moving water animals. When they change into adult frogs and toads, they start munching on worms and large insects. Toads are some of our best friends in the garden—because of all the mosquitoes and other pesky bugs they eat. It is estimated that one toad can eat 200 bugs in a single night!

▼ *A toad uses its sticky tongue to catch its dinner.*

**Largest frog:** Goliath frog, Africa; weight 7¾ pounds, length 3 feet

**Largest toad:** Cane toad, Latin America; more than 2 pounds

**Smallest frog:** Unknown! So many small species have not yet been discovered!

**Unusual frog tadpole:** Horned frog, Argentina, tadpoles are carnivorous.

**Fun fact:** The Flying frog of Southeast Asia jumps from high branches and glides through the air toward the ground.

The strawberry dart poison frog's bright colors warn predators that they are toxic.

## How far can a frog jump?

Frogs have been known to jump more than seven feet! Frogs have long legs made for jumping that they use to leap out of harm's way when predators threaten. People around the world are so fascinated by the jumping abilities of frogs that in many places, they hold frog-jumping contests.

## Are frogs and toads predators or prey?

You might be surprised to hear that frogs and toads can be predators. They eat invertebrates, fish, and even other vertebrates. The horned frog of South America, for example, has a mouth so big it can swallow birds! Small frogs, however, are often prey for big fish, snakes, and birds. To defend against predators, many frogs are active at night, can blend in with vegetation, or quickly leap away from danger. Some frogs that are not good jumpers have poisonous skin. The slime on South American dart poison frogs is so poisonous that it can paralyze or kill predators that lick it.

Many frogs are strong jumpers.

This toad uses its vocal sac to make sounds.

### Frog Serenades

Frogs, toads, and birds are some of the only groups of vertebrates we know of whose males use mating calls to attract females. Individual frogs have different songs. Female tungara frogs are attracted to male frogs singing songs that include two different kinds of sounds, called "whines" and "chucks." Meanwhile, female woodhouse toads like fast singers—the faster a male woodhouse toad can sing in a chorus, the more females he gathers around him! Larger male frogs and toads often have better songs—and some scientists believe that females listen to the songs and figure out which songs come from the biggest males. But what do females think is so great about a bigger mate? Well, scientists have found that, with bullfrogs, the larger males control the areas of ponds where water temperatures and vegetation are best for laying eggs.

# Life cycle of a frog

Most amphibians breed in water, where their eggs can stay moist as they develop. Because insects and fish are likely to eat the eggs, many amphibians lay eggs in places that are free of predators, such as puddles or plants that collect rainwater. Amphibians that lay their eggs in larger bodies of water often lay 5,000 to 10,000 eggs in one season! Laying large groups of eggs, called "egg masses," helps ensure that some of their young will survive. Eggs that eventually hatch will become tadpoles, which will change shape as they grow into adult amphibians.

I can't wait to grow up either!

## 1 Frog egg mass
Many frogs lay eggs in the water where they are fertilized. Frogs lay eggs in masses like this one, while toads lay eggs in strings. Both frog and toad eggs tend to look like clear jelly with dark polka dots in the middle.

## 2 Early development of embryo
The embryo develops within the egg into the tadpole stage. Once it has developed enough, it can move and break free of the egg using a tiny egg tooth to tear the thin membrane of the egg.

## 3 Newly hatched tadpole
This tadpole has hatched from its egg. Can you see its gills? Although tadpoles have no legs after hatching, their well-developed tail fins help them swim to avoid predators.

Will I look that different when I grow up?

### 4 Cluster of young tadpoles

There is safety in numbers—staying together helps individual tadpoles avoid being eaten if predators find them. Swimming in a group may also keep tiny tadpoles warm.

### 5 Tadpole starting to develop a hind foot

When frog and toad tadpoles reach a certain size, their shape and even their body parts start to change. This is called metamorphosis, which means "growing and changing." Metamorphosis is related to the long days of spring, which signal the arrival of warmer days and more food.

### 6 Tadpole with developed hind legs

Tadpoles develop their hind legs first. The front legs form, but they stay hidden under the skin behind the tadpole's head.

### 7 Tadpole with fully developed legs

This tadpole's front legs have emerged from its skin membrane and are almost fully developed. As the tadpole changes, it begins to look more like a frog and less like a fish

### 8 Tadpole with shortened tail

This tadpole's tail is being reabsorbed, and its lungs have developed. Metamorphosis happens quickly at high temperatures and moves along rapidly during the summer. For frogs that live in cold mountain ponds, metamorphosis can take years!

### 9 Adult frog

This adult frog has strong legs and no tail. It has changed from a partly vegetarian tadpole to a carnivorous adult frog. Its body shape, way of breathing, and behavior have all changed through metamorphosis!

# Salamanders

Of 300 known salamander species, almost two-thirds live in the Americas—mostly in the United States. Salamanders are amphibians that keep their tails as adults. These creatures can range in size from less than two inches to more than four feet long. Many salamanders breathe with lungs; others breathe through their skin. You might see adult salamanders in the woods—many live in ponds or streams.

## What do salamanders eat?

Although many salamanders are small, they play an important role in the food chain. They eat insects, worms, and leeches. Almost anything that's living in the salamander's damp habitat and is smaller, can become a very tasty meal!

## Is an eft a kind of salamander?

An eft is a young newt (one type of salamander) that spends most of its time on land. These dry-skinned amphibians can spend up to three years on land. After a few years, efts migrate together back to the ponds where they were born, then live in the water.

A salamander larvae in its egg

An axolotl with its feathery red gills

## What does the word "axolotl" mean?

In the Aztec language of Mexico, the word "axolotl" means "water monster." An axolotl is a form of tiger salamander. It keeps its gills into adulthood and lives underwater. Axolotls are usually gray in color but can also be albino.

**Largest salamander:** Asian giant salamander; over 5 feet long, 20 pounds

**Longest lived salamander:** Giant salamander; over 50 years

**Smallest salamander:** A Mexican salamander, Oaxaca state, scientific name "Thorius arboreus," less than one-inch long

**Highest-living salamander:** A Mexican salamander, scientific name "Psuedoeuycea gadovii," is found on the Orizaba volcano at over a 15,000-foot elevation!

**Fun fact:** Red salamanders and other lungless salamanders breathe through their skin.

Ha, ha, kid. Your fingers feel like a salamander ticklin' my neck!

# Are there any poisonous salamanders?

Yes. The fire salamander is probably the most famous poisonous salamander. Its bright yellow and black colors warn predators of its poisons, even at night when these salamanders roam the dark, damp woods.

# Where can I find salamanders?

Salamanders need moisture, so they hide under rocks, logs, or moss where it is damp. On spring nights after it rains, salamanders set up territories and mate, so they may be easy to find on wet roads, along streams, and in the wet woods.

*Aquatic salamanders, like these hellbenders, have loose skin.*

## Giant salamanders

Giant salamanders, with their long bodies, flat heads, and wrinkled skin, look quite bizarre. They might look mean, ugly, or dangerous, but there is nothing to fear; these strange-looking creatures are harmless. Waterdogs or mudpuppies, sirens, and hellbenders are all considered large salamanders.

### Are giant salamanders really giants?

If you compare them to other salamanders, they certainly could be called giants! Mudpuppies, for example, can be more than one foot long. Waterdogs, a kind of mudpuppy, grow to about eight inches long. Amphiumas, which live in swamps and ditches and are also called lamper eels or congo eels, can be almost four feet long! Hellbenders, the ugliest creatures in the group, grow to more than two feet long. Do they sound like giants to you?

# Snakes

Did you know that there are 2,700 kinds of snakes? All snakes are reptiles. Some of the world's biggest snakes—such as anacondas from South America and pythons from Africa and Asia—can be almost thirty feet long. These giant snakes eat large prey such as pigs or large rodents called "capybaras." They squeeze, or constrict, their victims and then swallow them whole!

Sssay sssweetheart, do you ssslither here often?

## What is a reptile?

Reptiles are cold-blooded vertebrates. There are many kinds, from sea turtles and crocodiles to snakes and lizards. Unlike moist amphibians, reptiles have dry skin, often covered with bony plates or scales. They lay watertight eggs or give birth to live young, so they can live far from water. **Nocturnal** reptiles, which are active at night, have good night vision but usually don't see in color. **Diurnal** reptiles, which are active during the day, have color vision.

## How many types of reptiles are there?

There are about 6,000 different species of reptiles!

▼ Boa constrictors and other snakes flick their tongues to smell their environment.

## Are snakes slimy?

Not at all! Since snakes are reptiles, they have dry, scaly skin that, to many people, feels a lot like leather. Snakes shed, or slough their skin, usually whole, a few times each year. How often a snake sheds depends on how fast they are growing, when they emerge from hibernation, or how many injuries or illnesses they've endured. When a snake is ready to shed, its eyes get cloudy, and it becomes irritable—probably because it cannot see well and feels vulnerable.

**Heaviest snake:** Anaconda, South America; can be over 300 pounds, twice as heavy as other boas or pythons its same length.

**Smallest snake:** Thread snake, West Indies; 4½ inches long

**Fun fact:** Pythons wrap their bodies around the clutch of eggs, twitching their muscles to create warmth.

Anacondas rest on branches above the water.

## How do snakes use their tongues?

Snakes have special tongues that help them find their prey and sense things in their environment. The tongues are not poisonous, as many people think. When the snake pulls its tongue into its mouth, it places it into a special area called the "Jacobson's organ," which helps the snake detect odors from the ground and air. Venomous snakes, use their tongue to follow the trail of a prey animal they have just injected with venom. The snake's tongue is split into a fork shape because this covers a wider surface area than a straight tongue. This allows them to follow the prey trail more easily.

## Are snakes deaf?

No. Even though snakes do not have external ear openings like we do, scientists have discovered they can hear some sounds that travel through the air. Snakes are better than cats at hearing the sounds of large animals moving nearby.

## What does a snake's skeleton look like?

Except for the skull, the snake's skeleton is made of a backbone of 150 to 450 vertebrae (compared with 33 in humans!). Each vertebra is attached to a pair of ribs. The snake's organs—the liver, kidneys, stomach, and intestines—are narrower and longer than the ones we have in our own bodies.

Snakes may not be deaf, but Kaa never listens to reason.

41

# Venomous snakes

Hissssss! While giant snakes kill their prey by squeezing them, venomous snakes kill or paralyze their prey with poison. Venomous snakes include cobras and sea snakes, as well as pit vipers such as copperheads and rattlesnakes. Pit vipers are named for heat-sensing pits they have in their faces which help them track warm-blooded prey. These creatures inject poison into prey through their fangs.

I'm ready to take on anyone who bothers me or Baloo!

Rattlesnakes shake their tails when they feel threatened.

## What is the killing power of one snake's venom gland?

An Australian tiger snake's venom could kill 118 sheep, and the Australian taipan has enough venom to kill 200 men. The Gabon viper also is highly venomous—a single bite from the viper can kill 20 people. And the sea snake's venom is even 100 times more deadly than that!

**Number of venomous sea snakes:** 40 different kinds, all members of the same family

**Number of eggs laid by cobras:** 20–40 eggs at a time

**Number of eggs laid by rattlesnakes:** None. Rattlesnakes give birth to live young.

**Continent with highest proportion of venomous snakes:** Australia, which has more than 70 kinds of snakes related to cobras

**Venomous snake prey:** Small mammals, birds, reptiles, frogs, and insects

## What's the biggest poisonous snake in the world?

The king cobra is the longest venomous snake on Earth. It can grow to be 18 feet long. The size of the eastern diamondback rattlesnake comes close to that of the king cobra—at only eight feet long. Cobras and eastern diamondback rattlesnakes are also some of the only snakes in which parents actively protect their young.

## How does venom work?

There are two kinds of toxins in venom. One toxin attacks the nervous system of the snake's prey; it's called "neurotoxin." The other attacks the blood system and is called "hemotoxin." Neurotoxins stop breathing muscles from working so that the victim suffocates; it also paralyzes heart muscles. Hemotoxins kill blood cells and damage the walls of blood vessels.

## Are there good uses for venom?

Actually, yes! Venomous snakes in captivity are "milked" for their venom, and small amounts are injected into horses. The horses produce antibodies that reduce the effect of the venom in their blood. Some of the horses' blood plasma is then used to cure humans suffering from snakebites.

## What's the fastest snake in the world?

One of the fastest snakes in the world is the poisonous black mamba from southern Africa. It can travel almost 15 miles per hour—that's almost as fast as a human can run!

Who needs venom? I prefer to ssssqueeze.

Cobras flare their hoods as they rear up to strike.

43

# Lizards

Lizards are a diverse group of cold-blooded reptiles that include bulgy-eyed chameleons, quick-running skinks, geckos, and the American ant-eating lizards we call "horned toads." They also include the spectacular frilled lizard of Australia, the common iguana of Latin America, the bizarre-looking Tokay gecko of Asia, and thousands of other amazing, scaly creatures, most of which have four legs and a tail.

Watch my lizardlike, lightnin' fast tongue eat this coconut.

▲ True chameleons, like this veiled chameleon, catch prey with their amazing tongues.

## What do lizards eat?

There are many different lizards in the world, with a range of appetites. The Komodo dragon eats vertebrates. Little anoles ("American chameleons" that live in Florida and other southern areas of the United States) eat insects. True chameleons catch insects with their long tongues. Iguanas eat fruits and vegetables, and horned lizards eat ants.

## What are the smallest lizards?

Geckos are among the smallest lizards. One, the helmeted gecko of Morocco from northwest Africa, is only three to four inches long. It spends most of its day under small balls of camel dung! The warmth and moisture there attract the tiny creatures it eats.

## What is a tuatara?

The tuatara looks like a lizard, but it is more ancient. It is a descendant of a group of animals that lived about 200 million years ago! This New Zealand reptile faces extinction because of introduced predators such as rats.

**Largest lizard:** Komodo dragon, Komodo and other Indonesian islands; up to 10 feet

**Smallest lizard:** A Caribbean Islands gecko, scientific name "Sphaerodactylus anasiae," discovered in 2001; less than one inch long

**Smallest chameleon:** Pygmy chameleon, Madagascar; 1¼–3 inches long

**Fastest lizard:** Racerunner, North America; about 20 miles per hour

**Number of lizard species:** About 3,500 worldwide

▲ Molochs may look tough, but they are really harmless.

## Do dragons exist?

Well, they don't breathe fire, but Komodo "dragons" are real, and they're the largest lizards in the world. They can grow up to 10 feet long!

## Can lizards really shed their tails?

Yes! A lot of lizards can shed their tail when danger threatens and just grow a new one later. In some American lizards, such as skinks, the young have bright blue tails that keep wiggling wildly even after they've fallen off! Scientists think this adaptation helps distract the predators and allows the wily lizards to escape.

Oh, I just hate the thought of losing my tail!

## Are there lizards that have no legs?

Yes. The glass lizard of North America and the slow worm of Africa, Europe, and parts of Asia are lizards that have no legs, or just very small legs. But, like other lizards, their tails may break off when a predator tries to grab them.

## Can geckos really walk up walls?

It's true! In fact, many geckos can even run across ceilings! Geckos can do this because they have thousands of clinging hairs on the bottom of each toe. These tiny hairs can even cling to surfaces as smooth as glass.

### Venomous lizards

There are only two kinds of venomous lizards, the Gila monster and the beaded lizard. They are close relatives, but the Gila monster lives on the ground, while the beaded lizard can climb trees.

The venom glands in these lizards are actually modified spit glands (salivary glands) at the sides of the lizard's mouth. When the lizard catches prey, venom flows along grooved teeth into the victim.

▲ Gila monsters are one of the only two kinds of venomous lizards.

# Crocodiles & alligators

*They don't scare me! But I'll stay away from them anyway.*

Crocodiles and alligators are descendants of the giant dinosaurs that once ruled the Earth and are now extinct. Alligators and crocodiles are the world's largest living reptiles, and they look very much alike. How can you tell them apart? When a crocodile shuts its mouth, the fourth tooth in its lower jaw sticks out.

## How long can crocodiles and alligators live?

Both reptiles can live for more than 50 years.

## Where are alligators and crocodiles found?

These large reptiles are found in swamps, lakes, rivers, and estuaries throughout the tropics and subtropics.

## How do alligators and crocodiles catch their food?

Alligators and crocodiles can move surprisingly quickly on land. They are also very fast and strong in the water, where they can hold their breath for up to 20 minutes! Alligators and crocodiles use their excellent swimming abilities to sneak up on prey from underwater. They stealthily make a rush to grab their prey, and if it struggles, they do a "death roll" over and over to drown their victim.

*And I thought Shere Khan had big teeth*

Freshwater crocodiles bask in groups and absorb heat from the sun.

## Why do alligators have such unusually shaped heads?

Alligators' eyes and nostrils both "bump up" out of the water as they swim. These feature allow the alligator to float motionless for hours, silently watching as its prey comes closer.

**Largest crocodile relative:** Saltwater crocodile, India to Australia (where it is called "Saltie"); more than 20 feet long

**Smallest crocodile relative:** Dwarf caiman, South America; less than 5 feet long

**Number of alligator and crocodile species:** 23

Alligators are well camouflaged predators.

Gavials have slender snouts.

## What is a gavial?

Gavials, or gharials, are fish-eating relatives of crocodiles. The word "gharial" comes from the word "gharas," which refers to the bump on the end of a male's snout. Gharial snouts are long and thin. Gharials live in larger rivers of India and surrounding countries.

## Do alligators and crocodiles take care of their young?

Alligators lay hard-shelled eggs in nests and guard these nests until the young hatch. Mother alligators often help their infants out of the egg, and then guard them against predators for several months—or even years! Learning about alligators' and crocodiles' parenting behavior helps us understand what kind of parents dinosaurs probably were.

A mother crocodile protecting her young.

47

# Turtles & tortoises

Turtles and tortoises are the only reptiles with **shells**. These creatures have a platelike bottom shell called a **plastron** and a protective upper shell called a **carapace**. Turtles' skeletons are unique because the bony plates that support their shells are built right into their backbones, and the creature's ribs are fused to them. When they're scared, turtles just pull their heads and legs into their protective shells.

My sssainted mother always ssssaid, "Respect your elders!"

## How many eggs do turtles and tortoises lay?

Some tortoises lay only one to eight eggs, while some sea turtles have been observed laying more than 200 eggs per group or **clutch.** Most turtles and tortoises lay their eggs in sandy soil. Depending on the species and surrounding temperatures, the eggs may take as few as four weeks or longer than twenty weeks to hatch.

▼ *One of the world's giant tortoises, an Aldabra tortoise, and a tiny speckled tortoise*

## How can you tell a male turtle from a female turtle?

In many turtle species, the male's tail is often longer. Most box turtle males have red eyes, while the females have brown eyes. But check out other parts of the body, too—females have flat plastrons, while males have concave plastrons, which curve inward.

## Is a matamata a turtle?

Yes! A matamata is a very bizarre-looking turtle. It is a member of the family of "snake-necked turtles," which live in South American swamps and rivers. Matamatas are brown, with many bumps on their shell and wrinkles or other leaflike projections in their skin that add to the turtles' leafy-looking camouflage. These turtles usually hide in the water, gobbling up small fish or other prey as the prey swim past.

**Largest land tortoise:** Galápagos tortoise, Ecuador Islands; 800 pounds, 4 feet long

**Largest freshwater turtle:** Temple turtle, China and Vietnam; more than 500 pounds, shell about 5 feet long

**Smallest African tortoise:** Cape speckled tortoise; shell less than 4 inches long

**Smallest American turtle:** Bog turtle; shell less than 4 inches long

## How did box turtles get their name?

Box turtles have very interesting shells, which have a hinge in the plastron that can be folded up against the edge of the carapace. Because their shells are tight and shaped almost like boxes, the turtles are called box turtles.

▼ *Galápagos tortoises are among the largest in the world.*

### Giant tortoises

Giant tortoises are land-dwelling tortoises found only on islands in the Pacific and Indian Oceans. Their shells can be almost four feet long, with remarkable domed carapaces, and they have large, stumplike legs that they can withdraw completely into their shells.

Giant tortoises, like many other turtles, live long lives. One Galápagos Island giant tortoise lived more than 175 years! These terrestrial tortoises tend to be much less carnivorous than their aquatic relatives. Giant tortoises eat plant materials, such as leaves, and cactus fruits, such as prickly pears.

# Sea turtles

Sea turtles live their entire lives in and around oceans. The leatherback turtle is the largest of all turtles and tortoises—its flippers can be up to eight feet from tip to tip! Over time, sea turtles have evolved into very large creatures, since seawater supports the weight of their bodies. Green sea turtles and loggerheads weigh hundreds of pounds. Their oarlike flippers make them well-suited for swimming.

I could go for a dip in the ocean myself!

## Is the snapping turtle a sea turtle?

No. Snapping turtles are in their own turtle family. Snapping turtles are most often found in freshwater. The largest snapping turtle is the alligator snapper of the Mississippi River basin—it lies in wait on the bottom of the river, wiggling a part of its tongue that looks like a worm. This attracts fish that the turtle eats.

Alligator snapping turtles lie in wait for their prey.

The sssight of me makes sssome hold their breath!

## How long can turtles stay underwater?

Some turtles can stay underwater for long periods of time. They don't need to take as many breaths as mammals do, because they do not use as much oxygen. Many turtles also have the ability to stay underwater even longer—they can take oxygen out of the water and absorb it into their bodies through special areas on their skin. They can even hibernate in the mud at the bottom of a pond for months.

**Largest sea turtle:** Leatherback or luth, worldwide in temperate or warm seas; weight 650–1,300 pounds, 6 feet long

**Smallest sea turtle:** Olive ridley sea turtle, Atlantic, Pacific, and Indian Oceans, tropical and subtropical waters; Kemps ridley, mostly Gulf of Mexico; 75–100 pounds, 2 feet long

**Web site:** www.cccturtle.org (Caribbean Conservation Corporation)

**Diet:** Sea jellies and ocean plants

Sea turtles have winglike flippers that help them swim.

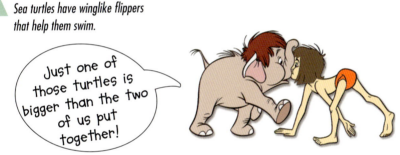

Just one of those turtles is bigger than the two of us put together!

## How do baby sea turtles hatch?

Unlike baby crocodiles that are helped to emerge from eggs by their mothers, baby turtles break the eggshell themselves using a bony structure called an "egg tooth." Baby turtles usually break out of their shells at night after a rainstorm or when it is cool outside, then burst out of the nest in a group and head toward the water.

## Where do baby sea turtles go after they enter the water?

It's not an easy ride! Many do not make it into the water fast enough, and are eaten by crabs or birds. Even in the water, they can still be prey to big fish or birds. In the ocean, they also can be caught in seaweed clumps or carried by ocean currents for years before they return home to their nesting beaches. Only about one in every 1,000 baby sea turtles survives.

Sea turtles lay their eggs on the beach after sundown.

### Nesting behavior

When a female sea turtle is ready to lay eggs, she finds her way, alone, to the nesting beach where she was born many, many years earlier. There, she will dig a nest cavity and lay her eggs. Then she uses her rear flippers to push sand back over the nest to protect it.

51

# Reptiles: Fascination & Fear

Man–cub, your connection to civilization is very important!

Throughout the ages, reptiles and amphibians have been more revered—and feared—than any other animals. They come in all sorts of strange shapes, colors, textures, and sizes. You might be able to spot them right in your backyard, or you perhaps never see them because they live only in exotic, faraway places. Some can walk on walls—others don't even have legs! It's no wonder that these creatures can be some of the most exciting—and frightening—on Earth! Let's take a look at a few of the most intriguing reptiles and amphibians out there.

## SNAKES: CURIOUSSSS OR SSSSCARY?

Sssss. Imagine a slithering snake, slowly moving toward you. It stops and coils itself. You see the smoothness of its scales, watch its forked tongue flick in and out of its mouth, and hear that unmistakable hisssss. Are you afraid? Curious? Perhaps you should consider this creature a little more closely.

Snakes have been on the planet for millions of years. Considering the fact that these animals are cold-blooded, legless, and have pretty poor eyesight, that's quite an amazing feat, don't you think? Snakes rely on their sense of smell, unlike people, who depend much more heavily on their senses of sight and hearing to survive.

For thousands of years, people have told stories—called myths— about different reptiles and amphibians. But did you know that there are more myths about snakes than about any other animal? There's the snake that appears in the Garden of Eden in the famous Bible story. Snakes also are very popular symbols in Egyptian culture; ancient Egyptians believed that some of the most important gods in their religion would take on the form of a snake. Serpents even play a role in Aboriginal legends and Norse mythology.

Clearly, you can tell that people from all over the world consider the snake a pretty interesting living thing—even though not everyone is a big fan of this legless reptile!

▲ Many-headed cobras are symbols of good fortune in Asian cultures.

## CROCODILES

Check out those jaws! No one wants to mess with a croc, that's for sure. You've probably heard stories about crocodiles and their sneaky surprise attacks. They're known just to lay still in the water and wait for unsuspecting prey, or they can run astoundingly fast on land. With those terrible-looking teeth, massive snouts, and strange-looking skin, they're yet another animal that inspires both fear and fascination!

Like snakes, crocodiles have been around for a very long time, and actually have changed little over the centuries—even since the age of the dinosaurs! We have come to learn that they are a very important part of the ecosystems in which they live. And the truth is, most crocodiles, such as the American crocodile, are actually on the shy side. They'd rather just stay away when it comes to being around people. If you think about it, humans might be considered even scarier predators. After all, adult crocs don't have any natural predators other than people. And today, many crocodile species are on the edge of becoming extinct because their habitats are being destroyed and because, for many years, people hunted crocs for their unusual skin.

So what do you think about these powerful beasts? Are they creepy, or cool?

▲ Nile crocodiles have fearsome grins.

▲ Don't try this at home! A girl kisses a frog, hoping for a prince.

## FROGS AND TOADS: WICKED AND WARTY OR PRINCELY AND PRECIOUS?

For a moment, think about what kinds of things you've heard about frogs and toads. You may have laughed at the silly story of the princess who kissed a frog—who then magically turned into a prince! And, have you ever heard that if you touch a toad, it would give you warts or poison you? There are all sorts of myths about frogs and toads.

Many of these wonderful little amphibians have long legs that are great for jumping, webbed toes, and a unique life cycle that transforms them from tiny tadpoles into tailless carnivores. Frogs and toads also make noises called "croaks," which you've probably heard on a summer night, or near a pond.

It may be that these stories about frogs and toads have their basis in the real magic these animals possess—the power of metamorphsis.

▲ *Great horned owl*

# Birds

Have you ever wished you could fly like a bird? You'd most certainly need feathers, wouldn't you? Birds, warm-blooded vertebrates that live all over the world, are the only animals on the planet that have feathers. Feathers grow out of their skin, and like scales on reptiles and fish, help protect it. They start growing as small bumps on the skin of the baby bird and form a pit, or **feather follicle**, for the shaft of the growing feather. Feathers do not grow all over a bird's body but in special areas of the skin called "**feather tracts**."

▲ *Mute swan*    ▲ *Peacock*    ▲ *Kingfisher*    ▲ *King condor*    ▲ *Ring-necked pheasant*

Feathers are light but surprisingly strong, and they serve different purposes, depending on where they are on the bird's body. Wing feathers help birds fly, while tail feathers help them turn, just as a rudder turns a boat. The feathers on a bird's body help control body temperature.

Birds live in a variety of habitats around the world. Each bird's feathers, bill, and way of protecting its young are well adapted for the climate and location in which it lives. Emperor penguins, for example, have waterproof feathers and use their body heat to insulate their chicks from the harsh Antarctic winter. Some birds are even adapted to live in different climates. They migrate in response to changes in the environment and weather. Many of these birds migrate huge distances every year. The artic tern (a sea bird) travels more than 25,000 miles annually!

Did you know that birds may be evolved from dinosaurs? Although you wouldn't think to associate a hummingbird with a T-Rex, the first birds evolved during the time of the dinosaurs, during the late Jurassic period. Scientists have even discovered fossils of species that appear to be a link, or a halfway point, between birds and dinosaurs. Maybe there is more to our feathered friends than meets the eye!

*Toco toucan* ▶

# Ostriches & relatives

Did you know that not all birds can fly? Unlike most species of birds, ostriches and their relatives have feathers designed not for flying, but for protection from the weather or for camouflage, and they have large leg bones built for running or kicking. Some ostriches live in the grasslands of Africa or Australia, while other relatives of the ostrich live in forests and eat either fruit or worms.

## Where do ostriches lay their eggs?

Ostriches and their relatives the rheas make scrapes in the ground to use as nests. Unlike many other birds, the male ostrich guards the eggs, sitting on them to keep them warm until the chicks hatch.

## How fast do ostriches run?

Adult ostriches can run 45 to 50 miles per hour—that's fast! Even month-old chicks can run 35 miles per hour! Since ostriches and their relatives cannot fly, they rely on their excellent vision and running abilities to avoid predators.

This cassowary's "helmet" helps it brush aside vegetation as it walks.

## Where do cassowaries and kiwis live?

The Australian cassowary and small New Zealand kiwi are both found in forest habitats. Cassowaries live by themselves and eat fruits, and kiwis travel alone at night and eat worms.

A kiwi searches for worms on the forest floor in New Zealand.

**Largest bird in group:** Ostriches can be over 8 feet tall and 300 pounds.

**Smallest bird in group:** Little spotted kiwi, 12 inches tall and about 2 pounds

**Best smeller:** Kiwi, whose nostrils in front of its long bill help it smell worms

**Strangest headgear:** Cassowary, whose tall, horny helmet helps it push dense vegetation out of the way as it moves through the rain forest

## Do ostriches sing or chirp like other birds?

Ostriches have a booming roar that sounds somewhat like a lion's roar. Emus make deep grunting sounds, and cassowaries have low coughs and make a piercing whistle sound at night, but they don't sing.

## How do ostriches sleep?

The way that birds rest and sleep is called "**roosting**." Ostriches and their relatives roost by sitting on the ground, resting their weight on their legs and chest, and nestling their head into their back feathers.

*Hmm, I wouldn't even sleep on the ground when I was camping with Mickey!*

### Enormous eggs!

Bird eggs come in many different sizes, shapes, and colors. Ostrich eggs are large, cream colored, almost round, and can weigh more than four pounds! Emu eggs are not as large, but are some of the most beautiful in the animal kingdom. Birds that nest in hollow cavities usually have white eggs because it is hard for predators to find the nest, but birds that nest on the ground lay eggs that are camouflaged. That makes it harder for predators to see the eggs.

▼ *Adult ostriches are on the lookout for danger as they stay close to their chicks.*

# Ducks, geese & swans

Ducks, geese, and swans are perfectly suited for the water. With webbed feet made for paddling, they are amazing swimmers. They have a special way of landing called "**whiffling**"—they tip from side to side with their feathers spread wide and plummet downward until they are almost at the surface of a pond or lake. Then the feathers come back together to slow the bird's descent so that it can land gently.

*I'm ready to come in for another perfect landing!*

## Do ducks sleep?

Yes, they do, sometimes with one eye open. Scientists only know of a few groups of animals that can do this. Ducks and geese sleep with one eye open so they can spot predators. While one-half of their brain sleeps, the other half remains awake to keep watch for the first sign of a predator. That way, they can make a quick getaway into the sky. Some mammals, such as dolphins, can also sleep with one eye open; they do it near the surface of the water so they can sleep, swim, and breathe—all at the same time!

## Do geese and swans really mate for life?

Yes, swans and many geese mate for life. Swans need such a large territory to find the plant food they like and to raise their young that a pair of trumpeter swans will often claim an entire pond to raise their family, chasing away other swans that come too close. Female swans and geese tend the nest, while males patrol the area to protect the group.

## How do migrating birds navigate?

We know that pigeons and bees use the position of the sun to find their way, just as we know direction by the sun, rising in the east and setting in the west. Birds also use stars to guide them at night.

*These mallard ducklings have camouflage coloration.*

**Largest duck relative:** Male trumpeter swan; wingspan eight feet, two inches, 38 pounds

**Smallest duck relative:** Hottentot teal; less than 10 inches and ½ pound

**Most feathers of any bird:** Whistling swan, with more than 25,000 feathers!

**Most common duck relative:** Mallard duck, found all around the world

## Water off a duck's back

Duck feathers, just like other birds' feathers, are specialized to protect their bodies from bad weather. Waterbirds have more down feathers than most birds, and these special feathers help trap air under larger feathers, providing an insulating cushion of warm air.

Male ducks are called "drakes."

Have you ever noticed how water rolls off a duck's back? Waterbirds have large oil glands, called "preen glands." In ducks, these glands excrete fat and wax, which we used to think helped to waterproof the feathers—until one scientist tried an experiment. He prevented some ducks from putting the oils on their feathers—and their feathers remained waterproof! It seems that good feather structure is just as important for waterproofing as the special oils from the duck's preen glands.

## Why do geese fly in a V-formation?

Geese are strong fliers, but during long flights everybody needs a little help. In the V-formation, each bird benefits from the airstream created by the bird in front of it. That means it doesn't have to flap its wings quite so hard. The leader of the V-formation is often the eldest female, but that sometimes changes so leaders can rest.

V-formations make flying easier for geese and swans.

Unca Donald showed me how to fly—by making paper airplanes!

# Eagles, falcons & other birds of prey

All birds of prey, called "raptors"—including eagles and falcons—have powerful, strongly hooked bills for tearing meat. Their sharp claws, called "**talons**," are used to grip and kill prey. As you may know, raptors eat the meat of other animals. They have excellent eyesight, but their eyes are fixed in place, so in order to watch their prey as it moves, hawks and eagles need to turn their heads.

I wish I could see as well as a hawk can.

This European kestrel sits on a perch to watch for prey.

## How do falcons help people?

Different kinds of falcons eat different things, but they all help people by eating the small animals that we consider pests. For example, kestrels eat insects and mice, while peregrines and larger hawks swoop down into city streets and eat pigeons and vermin.

## What is a "kettle" of hawks?

A "kettle" is the name for a large group of raptors flying together. Some hawks, such as broad-winged hawks, fly together during migration in a kettle made up of hundreds of birds.

## What bird can fly the fastest?

Peregrine falcons have streamlined bodies and sharply pointed wings. They soar high in the sky and can dive at over 175 miles per hour to catch their prey. That's more than twice as fast as we go in a car on the highway! Slower birds like ducks and shore birds need to be on the lookout when speedy peregrines are around.

**Largest eagle:** Harpy eagle, with an 8-foot wingspread and weighing more than 20 pounds

**Smallest hawks:** Black-thighed falconet, 5½–6½ inches, weighing 1–2 ounces

**Best vision in the animal world:** Peregrine falcons can see a white handkerchief 5,100 feet away.

# What is an "eagle"?

An eagle is a very large hawk. The wingspan on a soaring bald adult is six to seven feet across! Adult bald eagles weigh just eight to fourteen pounds, although females are larger than males (as is the case with most birds of prey). Bald eagles, which can fly when they are just two months old, mate for life and can live more than 30 years. Year after year, bald eagles return to the same nest, adding material to it each year—some old nests are more than 20 feet tall and weigh more than one ton! These eagle and falcon nesting places are often called "aeries" or "eyries."

I love looking to see if I can spot an eagle flying.

It's dinnertime, and a bald eagle swoops down from the sky to catch a fish.

# Parrots

Parrots have large bills that can open nuts and other foods they like to eat. The parrot's bill also acts as a third "foot" that parrots use as a helpful hook as they climb around in trees. Parrots have grasping feet they use for climbing, handling food, and perching. Some parrots, such as South American macaws, are strong fliers. Others, like kakapos of New Zealand, usually walk around.

Gee, some of these birds could out-talk Donald!

## Can parrots really talk?

Parrots have a voice box structure called a "syrinx" between their windpipe and lungs. When parrots breathe out, air travels through the syrinx and creates a series of sound waves with different pitches. Recently, scientists found that the parrot's large tongue acts just as our tongue does—little changes in its position lead to big changes in the sounds coming out. (Try to say "Polly want a cracker?" while you hold your tongue between your front teeth. Now say it again and concentrate on how your tongue is moving. Do you feel the difference?) The parrot's tongue helps turn bird squawks into what sound like words.

## What makes parrots so colorful?

Many parrots, parakeets, and macaws have feathers in beautiful, vibrant colors. In some birds and fish, the colors, or **pigments**, that show up in their feathers or scales are produced from the types of foods they eat. These colors are found in different parts of their bodies as well. But parrots actually produce their own unique red pigment just to color their feathers. This pigment isn't found anywhere else in nature!

▼ Parrots' large bills are perfect for opening nuts.

**Largest parrot:** Hyacinth macaw, which is 39 inches long and weighs over 3½ pounds

**Smallest parrot:** Pygmy parrots of New Guinea and nearby islands; only 3–4 inches long

**Coldest parrot habitat:** The New Zealand kea lives in snow-capped mountains.

▲ *Scarlet macaws and other parrots are excellent fliers.*

# Penguins

Penguins do not fly, but can swim through the water at speeds of up to 30 miles per hour. Penguins can walk upright for miles and when snow conditions are just right, they also can get around by pushing themselves along on their bellies with their webbed feet. Penguins' coloring is very distinctive; they have black backs and white bellies. These colors help camouflage them from predators.

*I thought all birds could fly!*

## Why do penguins walk in single file?

Penguins have legs that are set way back on their bodies so that they can stand up and walk. But, because they are a bit awkward on land, you may often see them walk in single file—following a leader makes walking a little easier for them.

## Why do penguins look so shiny?

Penguins are shiny because their feathers are very fine. They also have large preen glands, which produce oil that the birds work into their feathers. These waterproof feathers help penguins swim.

## What do you call groups of penguins?

Penguins live in groups we call "colonies" or "**rookeries**." For protection, young penguins stay together in groups called "**crèches**."

**Largest penguin:** Emperor penguin of Antarctica, which stands over 3 feet tall and weighs more than 85 pounds

**Smallest penguin:** Little blue penguin; less than 1 foot tall and only 2 to 3 pounds

**Fun fact:** Most penguins make loud trumpeting calls. Little blue and African penguins sound like loud donkeys.

*Emperor penguins and their chick in their frozen Antarctic habitat*

Adelie penguins heading off to find fish

## How deep can penguins dive?

Scientists have recorded emperor penguins diving to more than 1,650 feet (more than one-quarter mile!) below the surface of the ocean. Compare that to a human dive—without diving gear, the human world record is only 531 feet!

## Do all penguins live in Antarctica?

No. There are almost 20 penguin species, only a few of which live in Antarctica. Many are found in the southern oceans around New Zealand, South America, the Falkland (Malvinas) Islands, and South Africa. Penguins even live in tropical areas; there, they often live in burrows or shade during the day and have bare patches of skin that help them shed heat.

These birds have great fashion sense!

African penguins at their local beachfront habitat

65

# Pheasants, wild turkeys & peafowl

*Let pheasants run! A girl like me prefers a more leisurely stroll.*

Several different types of pheasants live around the world. These birds live in a variety of different habitats, where they eat an assortment of plant materials. All pheasants are ground-dwelling birds, and some are the ancestors of domestic chickens and turkeys. They are good runners and rarely fly, unless they need to escape from a predator or find a roosting spot high in the trees.

## Do pheasants eat the same food all year long?

Pheasants change their diets with each season depending on what is available. They often eat fresh leaf buds, grasses, and small insects in the spring, but will switch to munching on fruits, seeds, leaves, and other insects in the fall. Some even eat flowers when they can find them.

## How do turkeys avoid predators?

Turkeys not only have great eyesight, they are also very watchful birds. They often run when danger approaches, and, if a predator gets too close, they can fly away. Both turkeys and their relatives, such as Guinea fowl and peacocks, roost in trees at night to avoid predators.

*Ring-necked pheasants like this one live in grassy habitats around the world.*

▼ *Male, or "Tom," turkeys displaying their great tails*

**Largest pheasant relative:** American turkey; weighing more than 35 pounds

**Longest pheasant relative:** Peacocks may be the longest if you include their beautiful, 5-foot-long tails.

**Largest feathers of any wild bird:** The tail feathers of the crested argus pheasant

**Smallest pheasant relative:** Asiatic blue quail, which is less than 5 inches long and weighs less than 1 ounce!

**Loudest pheasant relative:** A turkey's gobble can be heard up to two miles away!

## Do turkeys make any noise besides gobbling?

Turkeys have over 25 different calls, including yelps, clucks, whistles, and even drumming sounds, in addition to gobbles. Turkeys are social birds and recognize the voices of many different individuals.

## Why do peacocks have such beautiful feathers?

When female peafowl, called "peahens," are looking for a potential mate, they tend to find male peacocks with long, beautiful tail feathers more attractive. The peacocks often fan their tails to show them off to the ladies. Having a tail that's too long and beautiful can be dangerous for the peacock, however, since heavier tails make it harder to get away from predators!

### Sacred birds

Some peafowl—which include peahens and peacocks—live on and around the Indian subcontinent. There, they serve as an important religious symbol to Hindus and Buddhists, who consider them sacred. In addition, the peafowl is the national bird of India, and so it is common to see this bird not just in forests, but also in villages and near temples in India.

A peacock calls loudly while showing off his brilliant tail.

# Owls

Have you ever heard the sound "*Hoo hoo!*" in the forest? You probably were listening to an owl. Owls are nocturnal creatures that fly silently so that they can hear the sounds of small prey and swoop down on them undetected. There are over 200 species of owls. These hunters have strong, hooked beaks, as well as a circle of feathers called a **"facial disk"** around each eye, which helps channel sound into their ears.

*Some owls rest in old trees and cavities like this one.*

## Where do owls nest?

Unlike many birds, owls do not build their own nests. Instead, they use a wide variety of nesting sites that might seem a little unusual. Large owls, such as great horned owls, make use of stick nests built by other birds, such as crows or hawks, or nest on cliff ledges. Some owls nest on the ground—or even underground! Burrowing owls, for example, nest in tunnels made by prairie dogs or other rodents. Many small owls may nest in tree cavities made by woodpeckers or squirrels, while owls in city parks have been known to nest in boxes!

## How do owls find their prey in darkness?

Owls' facial disks help direct the sounds of mice or other small prey to their very sensitive ears. They also have large eyes that help them see their prey in the dark. These eyes take up so much room in an owl's head that it cannot move its eyes. Instead, the owl needs to turn its head all the way to the back to see what's moving behind it!

## What do owl eggs look like?

Owl eggs are pure white, regardless of whether the owl's nest is in view of predators. Owl species that nest in cavities typically lay eggs that are round, since there is less chance the eggs will roll away and break.

## What do owls do during the daytime?

Most owls spend the daytime perched quietly in a hiding place, like a cave, the hollow space in a tree, or some other secluded place, where they are difficult to spot—even though they might be able to see you! These roosts help them hide from predators and protect them from bad weather.

**Largest owl:** Eagle owl, which is over 2 feet tall and weighs more than 8 pounds; It's about 100 times heavier than the littlest owl, the elf owl of North America.

**Smallest owl:** Elf owl, which is less than 5 inches long and weighs less than 2 ounces

**Biggest owl egg:** Eurasian eagle owl, 2 inches

**Smallest owl egg:** Elf owl, 1 inch, with a clutch of 2–4 eggs

**Fun fact:** Female owls tend to be larger than males.

## What is an owl pellet?

Owls eat small animals whole. An owl pellet is made up of the undigested fur, bones, teeth, and other items left over from the owl's last meal. Since the owl cannot digest this material, it's compressed into a sausage-shaped "pellet" that the owl "coughs" up. Scientists can tell what owls eat by dissecting their pellets; they've found that some barn owl families can eat more than 100 rats a month!

▼ A barn owl is ready to catch a mouse in its powerful talons.

Hey, for these birds, having a 'big bill' doesn't cost a thing!

# Big-billed birds

Hornbills and toucans hop far out on the branches of tropical forest trees, then use their long bills to collect fruits that other animals cannot reach. They digest the fruits, but spread the seeds around the forest, which makes new trees grow! Related birds with large bills, such as kingfishers, kookaburras, ground hornbills, and bee-eaters, are experts at catching and eating fish, frogs, snakes, and insects.

## Where do big-billed birds nest?

Most of these birds nest in cavities—either in crevices that are already available, or cavities in trees or stream banks that the birds dig out themselves. When female hornbills lay eggs, their mates seal the cavity's entrance until only a tiny slit remains—the male feeds her through this slit as she sits on the eggs. Such small holes help protect baby hornbills from snakes and other predators.

## Do kingfishers really "fish"?

Many kingfishers are "sit-and-wait" hunters that perch close to a stream or the surface of a pond. They watch for the movement of prey in the water or on the shore, then swoop down and grab the prey in their bill. Some kingfishers can hunt while hovering above the water—then they dive into the water to snatch a fish!

▲ Kingfishers often wait for fishing opportunities from streamside branches.

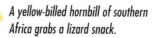

▲ A yellow-billed hornbill of southern Africa grabs a lizard snack.

**Largest hornbill:** Helmeted hornbill, which can be more than 4 feet tall and weigh more than 6½ pounds!

**Smallest hornbill:** Red-billed dwarf hornbill, which is only about 1 foot long and weighs about 3 ounces

**Smallest kingfisher:** African dwarf kingfisher, which is just 4 inches long and weighs less than 1 ounce!

**Largest kingfisher:** African giant kingfisher, 18 inches long and almost 1 pound

*This South American Toco toucan is more than 20 inches long.*

## Hummingbirds

Hummingbirds from the Americas and sunbirds from Africa and Asia also have very long bills. These birds feed on the high-energy, sugary solution found deep within flowers, by hovering in front of the flower and using their slender bills and long tongues to collect the nectar. Have you ever seen a hummingbird suspended in front of a flower? They are such good fliers that they can even fly backward—while their wings beat more than 70 times per second!

The smallest bird in the world is the bee hummingbird, which is only two inches long and less than one-tenth of an ounce.

The smallest egg laid by any bird is less than one-half of an inch long. It's laid by the tiny woodstar hummingbird, which lives in South America.

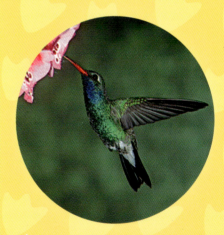

*A broad-billed hummingbird hovers by a flower.*

# Vultures

Vultures are raptors, but instead of hunting, they serve as nature's cleanup crew—they clean up, or **scavenge**, dead animals called "**carrion**." Vultures have strong beaks used to tear animal flesh. They are some of the highest-flying animals in nature; they use warm air currents called "**thermals**" to gain altitude as they search for food. The condor, a vulture relative, has a ten-foot wingspan—the largest of any bird.

King vultures of South America are New World vultures.

## Are all vultures the same?

Not exactly. Vultures in Europe and Africa are related to hawks and eagles, while vultures in the Americas are more closely related to storks. But they have similar features, which help them fulfill their jobs as scavengers. Both types of vultures also have broad wings that allow them to soar high above ground.

## How do vultures find their food?

Old World vultures from Europe and Africa find dead animals using their excellent vision—one vulture sees the carcass and begins circling slowly downward toward it. Other birds see its downward circling and join from miles around. New World vultures, such as turkey vultures in North and South America, have a well-developed sense of smell. This allows these vultures to find food even in heavily wooded areas. They also circle slowly downward toward the carrion, allowing other kinds of vultures and condors to see them and join in. Each vulture species does a different job on the carrion—ripping the skin or hide, tearing into the muscle, or even trying to break and eat bones!

**Bald is beautiful**

Many vultures are known for their naked heads. As vultures eat dead animals, they sometimes have to stick their heads right into the bodies of the animals they're eating. So, you can imagine why it might be good that their heads are naked. Even though they might look a little strange, they probably keep their heads a lot cleaner than they would if they had feathers.

**Smallest vulture:** American black vulture; 23 inches and 2–3 pounds

**Largest vulture:** Andean condors can weigh more than 30 pounds.

**Number of eggs:** Vultures lay 1–3, but normally 2, eggs.

**Highest vulture flight known:** Andean condor, which can reach an elevation of 20,000 feet!

Ack! If I can't find my way out of here soon, the vultures will find me!

These Andean condors' bald heads make feeding on carrion clean and simple.

## What is the most impressive vulture relative?

The condor has a wingspan of ten feet—the largest of any bird, even bigger than the seven-foot wingspan of the bald eagle, and about 30 times wider than the four-inch wing-spread of a hummingbird. That's one big bird!

## Where do vultures nest?

Vultures do not build nests of their own, but lay eggs directly on rock ledges, in caves or the hollows of large trees, or even on the ground. Because vulture chicks aren't able to take care of themselves until they are several months old, both parents may sit on the eggs and take care of the chicks after they hatch.

California condors like this one were once almost extinct but are making a comeback due to conservation efforts.

# All About Beaks

Well, this is certainly a good looking bunch!

In addition to feathers and wings, what else does every bird have? A beak! Beaks are also called bills. Have you ever noticed that birds' beaks come in all shapes and sizes? If you take a look at the birds here, you'll see many different beaks and bills.

Beaks and feathers—even your own hair and nails—are made up of keratin, which is flexible but strong. It allows birds to use their beaks or bills to do their most important job—eat! Birds have no teeth, so they use their beaks to collect and eat food. How does the shape of each bird's beak featured here reveal what kind of food it eats?

## WHAT IS A HOOKED BEAK GOOD FOR?

Eagles, hawks, owls, and other birds of prey have hooked beaks. A hooked beak works like the knife you use to cut your meat at dinnertime. These birds use their beaks to tear their prey's flesh into pieces they can swallow. Although owls often swallow small prey whole, they still use their sharp beaks on larger prey, such as skunks.

*Eagle* ▶

## WHY DOES THAT LITTLE BIRD HAVE SUCH A LONG BEAK?

The hummingbird's beak is like a straw with a long tongue inside. It is designed to help these tiny flying birds reach deep inside flowers and sip nectar.

◀ *Hummingbird*

## HOW DO WATERBIRDS EAT WITHOUT SWALLOWING A LOT OF WATER?

Some waterbirds, such as ducks and geese, have special bills that work like strainers. You've seen how a spaghetti strainer removes water and leaves the spaghetti behind, right? Well, when a duck eats, its bill strains water out and leaves behind the small plants that the bird plucks from the water.

*Duck* ▶

## WHAT KIND OF FOOD DOES THIS BIG-BILLED BIRD EAT?

Macaws and other birds with bills curved like this eat different kinds of nuts. They use their big bill like a nutcracker. With beaks like this, the bigger the beak, the bigger the nuts they can crack!

*Parrot* ▶

## WHAT DOES A WOODPECKER EAT WITH ITS BEAK?

A woodpecker's beak is shaped like an ice pick. It's perfect for drilling holes in trees—where there are lots of insects to eat!

◀ *Woodpecker*

## HOW DO SWALLOWS USE THEIR BEAKS?

Swallows and birds with similar beaks use their beaks like funnels. The swallow's beak is surrounded by hairy feathers, which help guide tiny insects into the bird's mouth.

*Swallow* ▶

## HOW DOES THIS BIRD USE ITS LONG POINTY BEAK?

That's one pointy beak, isn't it? Herons use it to catch fish. This spearlike beak acts more like a pair of kitchen tongs than a spear. The heron lunges after fish with its beak partially open. Once it has caught a meal, its beak snaps shut and pulls the fish out of the water.

◀ *Heron*

## HOW CAN A TOUCAN EAT ANYTHING WITH A BEAK THAT BIG?

Even though the toucan's beak is very large, it isn't heavy. Its long, lightweight beak comes in handy because it lets the bird pluck hard-to-reach fruits from trees. It's also helpful when the bird is eating fruits that are sticky, since it can eat and still keep its feathers clean.

*Toucan* ▶

# Insects

Buzzzzz ... Have you ever seen a wiggly little critter under a rock, or heard a bee buzzing in the garden? Bugs are those small animals we rarely see, although sometimes we notice them because of their fascinating colors, trilling songs, or painful bites and stings. Even though bugs are usually quite small, as a group they outnumber and outweigh all the bigger animals in the world put together!

What is a bug? "Bugs" are what we commonly call insects. Not all insects are bugs, however. True bugs are actually only one type of insect.

▲ Garden spider    ▲ Wood ants    ▲ Scorpion    ▲ Grasshopper    ▲ Caterpillar

Insects are in a category of animals called arthropods (which means "jointed feet"), along with lobsters, crabs, scorpions, and spiders. Insects are diferent from these other creatures, however, because their bodies are divided into three sections—a head, a thorax, and an abdomen. Plus, as adults they all have six legs on their thorax. Many insects, such as beetles, butterflies, and mosquitoes, have wings as adults. In fact, insects were the first animals to develop flight millions of years ago.

Unlike humans, who have skeletons on the insides of our bodies to give us support, arthropods have shell-like support structures called "exoskeletons" on the outsides of their bodies. "Exo" means "outside," and "skeleton" means "support structure." Exoskeletons help protect the arthropods' bodies. When you go biking, boarding, or skating, you wear arm pads, knee pads, and a helmet to protect your body, right? An arthropod's exoskeleton works similarly. If you look closely, you can see that arthropods, such as beetles and other bugs, have special outer coverings. The inner layer of these coverings is living, while the outer layer is a hard "cuticle." Although the helmets and protective pads we wear are made of plastic and other manmade materials, the cuticles of bugs are made of proteins and a tough material called "chitin," which each insect produces.

Bugs are all around us—in hot places and cold places, in jungles and even jumping around in snow! They can be beautiful or ugly, dangerous or helpful. There are more than 750,000 species of insects, 73,000 species of spiders and their relatives, plus another 50,000 kinds of arthropods. Scientists estimate there are millions more that haven't even been discovered!

*Walking stick* ▶

# Beetles

Being a ladybug doesn't automatically make me a girl! You got that?

There are more beetles in the world than any other kind of insect—more than 350,000 species! You can identify a beetle by its chewing mouthparts, its forewings, which are thickened so that they work as a type of shield, and its large hindwings, which fold under the beetle's forewings. Beetles come in a variety of sizes from very small to very large, and are found in all habitats around the world.

## Do beetles help us?

Beetles are very valuable in our world's habitats because they clean up debris and prey on pest insects. For instance, our garden friends, the ladybird beetles (you might call them "ladybugs"), prey on aphids and other insects that are harmful to human activities. Some beetles even clean up poop! Dung beetles roll it away to eat or to feed their larvae.

## What is a beetle's best defense against predators?

To defend themselves, some beetles bite, while some make an audible clicking noise. Others, like the bombardier beetle, use chemicals. If it is forced to defend itself, the bombardier beetle squirts out a mix of hot, irritating chemicals into its predator's face!

## How are beetles different from true bugs?

There are about 55,000 species of bugs. Beetles chew; bugs have sucking mouthparts used mostly for feeding on plants. Bugs also hold their wings flat or tented over their bodies when they are resting, unlike beetles. Types of bugs include stinkbugs, bedbugs, leafhoppers, and cicadas.

▼ A dung beetle rolls up a nutritious morsel of dung for its larvae.

**Heaviest insect:** Goliath beetle, which lives in Africa; 3.5 ounces and 6 inches

**Smallest insect:** They're so small you probably wouldn't see them, but feather-winged beetles and fungus beetles are less than 1/50 inch long —smaller than a pinhead!

Do red and black look like girlie colors to you?

Male stag beetles use their huge jaws to wrestle rivals.

I'm really big in the circus world.

## How do beetles grow?

Beetles go through a life cycle called "complete metamorphosis." Adult beetles lay **eggs** that hatch, and a **larva**, or grub, emerges. Larvae grow and molt several times, then produce a **pupa**. Soon after, the beetle becomes a winged adult!

## How are beetle grubs different from flying adults?

Larvae are wormlike and have mouths specialized for feeding, whereas adult beetles—with their wings—are well adapted for flying around to find new places to live, eat, and mate.

Ladybird beetles prey on garden pests.

79

# Flies & mosquitoes

There are many different kinds of flies. They all have one pair of true wings, unlike other insects, which have two sets of wings. Small flight organs behind the wings, called "halteres" help them balance when they fly and even when they land upside down on ceilings. Flies such as the hover fly serve as our friends in the garden—their larvae feed on insects that we consider pests.

We may only be here for a short time but we know how to live it up!

Flies have only one pair of true wings.

## Are flies helpful to people?

Yes and no. The larvae of lots of flies are called "maggots." They feed on dead or dying plant and animal materials, which helps rid the environment of decay. However, maggots can sometimes cause problems for people by eating vegetable or fruit crops. The fly you probably know the best is the common housefly. Many humans consider the housefly a pest because it carries lots of germs on its feet.

## Are mosquitoes members of the fly family?

Yes. Their larvae, called "wigglers," are found in water. The larvae hatch in about five days and breathe from underwater through a built-in breathing tube. When they become adults, mosquitoes only survive for a few weeks— just enough time to start the whole cycle over again. Swarms of mosquitoes do not make us happy, but they do serve as food for bats and birds!

## What is the mosquito's natural enemy?

Dragonflies! Dragonflies and their relatives, the damselflies, love to munch on mosquitoes. Although adult dragonflies live only one to eight months, their larvae can live underwater for years before they become adults. So, adult dragonflies are eating up adult mosquitoes, while dragonfly larvae devour as many mosquito wigglers as they can find in the water.

**Largest fly:** Crane fly; 2½ inches long

**Heaviest fly:** South American robber fly; 2 ounces

**Most eggs:** Crane fly; almost 2 inches long and lays 1,000 eggs at a time!

**Most unusual fly:** Tiny bat fly, which lives on bats, and has no wings of its own

## What is the deadliest animal in the world?

Believe it or not, the tiny mosquito is the deadliest animal of all! According to the World Health Organization, female mosquitoes can spread diseases such as malaria and West Nile virus when they bite people, killing more than 2.5 million people every year.

A female mosquito fills up on a meal of blood.

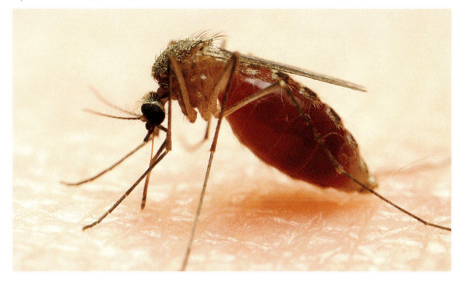

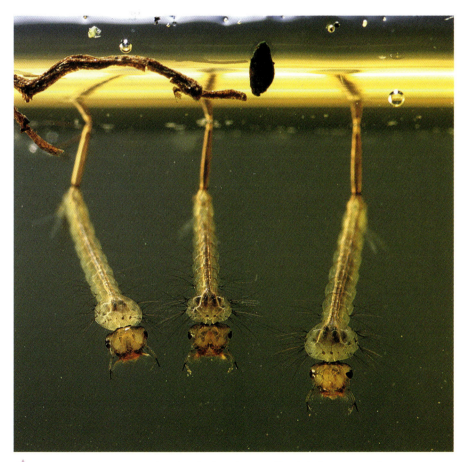
Tiny mosquito larvae, or wigglers, breathe through rear-end snorkels that penetrate the water surface.

## Can mosquitoes hear their own buzzing?

With its antennae, a male mosquito can hear the whirring of a female's beating wings one-quarter mile away!

Wow! Mosquitoes would make great warriors!

## Why do mosquitoes bite people?

Mosquitoes and other biting flies do not see or sense the world the way people do. Mosquitoes can detect both the heat that our bodies produce and the carbon dioxide that we give off when we exhale, and they are highly attracted to both. Each kind of mosquito flies actively and bites victims at particular hours, most often at dawn and dusk. Mosquitoes are also affected by the local temperature, the amount of moisture in the air, and the amount of light in the environment. Many mosquitoes are found only at certain heights above the ground. Mosquitoes do not care about the kinds of victims they bite, so if you are outdoors where and when they are active, you are likely to be bitten!

Just 19,999 trips to go!

# Bees & wasps

Have you ever heard the saying "busy as a bee?" It's based on the fact that honeybees are very busy! They make thousands of trips to flowers to get nectar and pollen, which they use to make honey. Scientists believe it takes 20,000 one-mile trips for one bee to make one pound of honey. So, if one bee made a whole jar of honey, it would have to fly 20,000 miles to do it—that's almost one trip around the Earth!

## What's the difference between honeybees and bumblebees?

Both start hives with a single queen, but honeybees make their hives above ground (often in a tree), while bumblebees make their hives underground. Bumblebees generally have larger, yellower bodies than honeybees and are active in cooler weather. Bumblebees can have colonies of up to 300 individuals; honeybee colonies are much larger, with up to 60,000 individuals.

Honeybees gather around their queen on the cells of a honeycomb.

## Are bees and wasps different?

While wasps can sting you many times, bees sting just once, lose their stinger, and then die. Another difference is that many wasps, such as paper wasps and mud-dauber wasps, make nests of paper or mud. Bees, like honeybees and bumblebees, make the cells in their nests with wax produced in their bodies. Bees use plant pollen and flower nectar to make honey, which is fed to growing larvae, while wasps are predatory and feed the insects they capture to their young. Almost all wasps die during the cold winter, but some queens survive to produce more colonies the next year.

**Largest wasp:** Tarantula hawk wasp, which can grow up to 2 inches long

**Largest bee:** The Malayasian leaf-cutter bee can grow up to 2 ½ inches long.

**Largest honeybee in colony:** Queen bee

**Bee diet:** Nectar and pollen

**Wasp diet:** Other insects—of more than 130,000 wasps, bees, and ants, 100,000 are wasps that are parasites of other insects!

**Fun fact:** In a single colony, all worker bees are sisters!

## How do honeybees know where to find flowers full of nectar?

Honeybees returning to the hive tell their relatives about successful nectar-gathering trips by dancing! One of the bee's dances—the **round dance**—tells the others that flowers are close by, while another dance—the **waggle dance**—means that flowers are more than 50 yards away. The waggle dance is a circular motion on the wall of the hive, then a wiggle up the middle. The angle at which the bee moves up the middle tells the others where to find the flowers in relation to the sun!

▲ A wasp tending its property nest.

*My honey just found another flower!*

## How do bees make honey?

Honey is a concentrated solution of simple sugar and a little protein and salt. Bees sip up the watery nectar from flowers. Back at the hive, water evaporates from the nectar—what's left behind is honey!

▼ A pollen-covered bee hovers above a flower.

# Ants

Ants are related to wasps and bees. Some ants have wings, while others, which cannot fly, are usually made up of different groups including royalty, workers, and soldiers. The different members are very efficient in their efforts to create a nest and to feed and defend the colony, which can have more than half a million members!

I represent an ant colony!

## What's special about a leaf-cutter ant?

In the wild, leaf-cutters cut the leaves off more than 200 kinds of plants and take the leaf parts underground. There, the leaf parts are inoculated with a special fungus, and the new cuttings help the fungus grow. The ants then eat the fungus they've grown. They may be the best gardeners in the insect world!

## Can ants see well?

Since most ants live underground, they don't really have a need for good vision.

▼ Two leaf-cutter ants transport a leaf several times their size.

## What's the most destructive ant?

Although many ants are carnivorous, the most feared ants are probably driver ants of Africa or army ants of South America. The colonies of these ants make no nests but move every day and eat just about everything in sight. The ant "soldiers" are the hunters and defenders of the colony, while the "worker" ants take care of the larvae while the colony is on the move.

I can't wait to be able to fly!

**Largest ant:** Dinoponera grandis; South America

**Smallest ant:** One of the smallest is the "Thief ant" at $\frac{1}{32}$ inch; difficult to detect

**Ant diet:** Most ants are carnivorous.

## Can an ant's bite or sting kill you?

While all ants can bite with their jaws, some ants, such as South American bullet ants or fire ants, have very painful stings that release a nerve toxin. A sting from a bullet ant could paralyze your arm for days! Fire ants can be deadly. When a colony is disturbed, many fire ants attack all at once. They'll bite down on you first to get a firm grip and then deliver their sting. Ouch! People who are allergic to bee or wasp stings may also have a severe allergy to fire ants.

▼ A swarm of wood ants move a leaf.

## If ants can't see very well, how do they find their way?

Worker ants, which need to find their way to food and then back to the colony, lay down a scented trail from their abdominal glands as they move. Other ants follow this trail using the sensitive areas of their antennae.

Ants, like these nomad ants, use odor trails laid by other ants to find their way. ▶

▲ Weaver ant

### Amazing ants!

An ant can lift 20 times its body weight.

An ant has two stomachs—one holds food that it eats and one holds food that it shares with other ants.

An ant's brain has about 250,000 brain cells. A human brain has about 10 billion. So, if you were an ant in a colony of 40,000 ants, you would have the collective brainpower of one person!

Ants are tidy creatures. Some worker ants have the job of cleaning the colony and putting refuse outside the entrance holes. Since each colony has its own odor, intruders to the colony can be identified. They are attacked and removed with the rubbish.

Some ants spray an irritating material called formic acid to drive intruders away from the colony. Birds sometimes roll on the top of an anthill to make the ants spray formic acid. This helps them drive away parasites from their feathers!

# Butterflies & moths

There are over 170,000 species of butterflies and moths, found on all continents except Antarctica. Only 10 percent of these species are butterflies; most are moths. All species undergo metamorphosis through four stages of life: egg, larva (we call this a caterpillar), pupa (cocoon or chrysalis), and adult. Butterfly eggs are often deposited on specific plants that serve as food sources for their caterpillars.

*I stop the show with my metamorphosis act!*

## What do caterpillars eat?

Good question—caterpillars are always eating! They eat plant materials constantly, so they grow to hundreds of times their hatching size! When they are large enough, they spin a cocoon and stay inside without eating while the final stage of metamorphosis takes place. Inside the cocoon, the caterpillar turns into a beautiful, winged butterfly or moth.

## What are butterflies made of?

Butterflies actually have clear wings that are covered with tiny colored scales that overlap like shingles on a roof. These scales can rub off easily, leaving "colored powder" on your hands if you handle a butterfly or moth too roughly.

*This caterpillar munches on plants to help it grow.*

*Monarch caterpillars metamorphose into butterflies inside a chrysalis like this one.*

**Largest butterfly or moth:** Atlas moths and giant silk moths—with wingspans of over 12 inches, they're often mistaken for birds!

**Where silk comes from:** Silk moth caterpillars, used for over 4,500 years

**Do moths have ears?:** Yes; found in their wing roots, abdomen, or head

**Oldest moth:** Fossil from 140 million years ago

**What is a jumping bean?** A seed containing a moth caterpillar that "jumps" near heat.

## How do butterflies eat?

Many butterflies suck nectar from flowers through something called a "proboscis," a long, coiled mouthpart that butterflies use like a drinking straw.

## Do butterflies and moths do anything to help us?

All animals, even those we consider pests, play an important role in our environment. For example, when butterflies or moths drink nectar from a plant, they may pick up pollen and drop it onto the next plant, fertilizing it. Many butterflies and moths also are important in the food chain, although some, such as monarchs, develop chemicals inside their body that makes them taste bad to birds. Moths can be useful to humans, too. One of the most beautiful fabrics we have—silk—comes from moths.

## What is the difference between butterflies and moths?

Moths most often fly and feed at night, and butterflies fly during the day. Butterflies usually hold their wings vertically when at rest and have antennae that look like they have a little knob at the end. Moths, on the other hand, usually fold their wings around their bodies or spread them out when they rest. Their antennae are more threadlike or feathery.

Monarch butterflies are commonly observed sipping nectar from lilacs and other flowers.

### Monarch butterflies

Do you know what a monarch butterfly looks like? Its bright orange and black wings are well known in North America, where this butterfly appears in summer and fall, especially in fields where a plant called milkweed grows. When monarch caterpillars eat milkweed, they absorb a kind of poison from the plant. This poison doesn't kill them, but instead is stored in their bodies—then, as adult butterflies, they become poisonous to predators. If a bird eats a monarch, it will get sick from the effects of the toxin, and so learns to avoid eating other monarchs. One edible butterfly, called the viceroy butterfly, has wings with the same colors that monarchs' wings have—this tricks birds into not eating it!

The luna moth uses its antennae to detect the scent of faraway females.

# Insect jumpers

Let's ride!

Locusts, grasshoppers, crickets, and katydids all belong to the same order of insects. They are known for their leaping abilities and chirping sounds. Some of these insects chirp by rubbing their back legs against special areas of their wings, while others chirp by rubbing their wings together. These creatures also hear with receptors on their legs. This allows them to sense predators approaching and quicky escape.

## What's the difference between a grasshopper and a katydid?

One difference is that grasshoppers have short antennae, and katydids have long antennae that look like threads over their backs. Katydids also rub their wings together to make their chirping *"katy-did, katy-didn't"* call. Most katydids are green and blend in well with the vegetation where they hide and feed.

▼ *A well-camouflaged katydid shows off its very long antennae.*

▲ *Grasshoppers' large eyes help them see predators and avoid danger.*

**Largest jumper:** Australian giant grasshoppers are one of the largest at 3 inches long

**Smallest jumper:** Sand flea or chigo, which is less than 1 mm long

Grasshoppers have short antennae.

## How do fleas jump?

Fleas are parasites that move by crawling or jumping. Fleas can jump 200 times their own length—that's like a man jumping over a 70-story building! They leap and jump again in no time at all; one flea was observed jumping 600 times in an hour! How do they do it? When a flea gets ready to jump, it cocks its hind legs, squeezing a special, springy protein in its muscles, called "**resilin**." When the flea jumps, the resilin releases that stored energy all at once, and the flea catapults into the air! Fleas' legs also have hooklike bristles that catch onto the hair of the animal on which the flea lands. Because they have such amazing jumping abilities, fleas have been successful parasites for millions of years! Pesky little critters, aren't they?

Fleas are amazing jumpers.

## Are cockroaches related to katydids and grasshoppers?

They might not look like relatives, but they are indeed! Cockroaches are related to crickets, too. Cockroaches live in a variety of habitats, and the ones that live in human habitats can even survive by eating concrete and wood. There are about 55 cockroach species in North America. Cockroaches tend to stay away from light, so they're more often found in dark crevices.

## What is a flea's life like?

Fleas belong to a different order of jumping insects than grasshoppers. There are about 1,000 different kinds of fleas. The flea's ideal habitat is the hair or feathers of an animal; its food is the animal's blood. They live on animals of all kinds, but we are most familiar with the fleas that live on dogs.

I'm a black widow—widowed 12 times actually!

# Spiders & scorpions

There is a class of creatures, called arachnids, that many people think of as insects, but they aren't actually insects. This group includes spiders, scorpions, and other arthropods. Arachnids are a type of arthropod. Arachnids include spiders, scorpions, and mites, which all have two major body parts—an abdomen and a combined head and thorax.

## What do spiders eat?

There are more than 30,000 different kinds of spiders. Most of them eat insects, but some catch fish and other small animals that live in the water, or even small birds! They all have different ways of catching live prey. All spiders eat by sucking nutritious juices out of their prey. Many of them use spiderwebs to capture their prey, but some, such as jumping spiders and wolf spiders, use speed instead of webs.

## Are spiders dangerous?

All spiders are venomous, which means they must bite to inject their venom. Some spiders, like the black widow, are dangerous to humans. Most others, like garden spiders, are helpful to humans because they eat insect pests. Their venom is harmful only to the insects they prey upon.

Garden spiders spin their webs at night.

## Can tarantulas really throw their hairs?

Yes! Tarantulas have thousands of special hairs on their bodies. The tarantula can throw these hairs by flicking its legs on its abdomen. The hairs are very irritating and cause the attackers to itch wherever they land.

Red-kneed tarantulas are very distinctive. Can you see the hairs?

**Largest spider:** Goliath bird-eating spider, with a leg span of 11 inches and a weight of 4.3 ounces; found in South America

**Smallest arachnids:** Mites; one species is so small it lives in moths' ears!

**Best camouflage:** Crab spiders can change color to blend in with the flower on which they're sitting.

**Most dangerous to humans:** The funnel web spider has highly toxic and fast-acting venom.

## What is a daddy longlegs?

You might think a daddy longlegs (also known as a "harvestman") is a spider, but it's really another arachnid related to spiders. Daddy longlegs have eight legs just like spiders do, but only one body part instead of two. Spiders also produce silk, while daddy longlegs do not. A very old daddy longlegs was recently found encased in 100-million-year-old amber from Myanmar in Asia!

Come on, legs! Let's all go in the same direction.

A harvestman, or daddy longlegs

## Are scorpions insects?

No, they are arachnids, just like spiders, and there are about 600 different species. The largest scorpion is the emperor scorpion of Africa, which is several inches long. A scorpion can kill smaller animals with venom from its large stinging tail. Did you know scorpions glow green or purple under ultraviolet light? That's one way scientists find them at night out in the wild!

Caution! A scorpion shows its defensive posture.

# Millipedes & centipedes

I told the colony I could find bigger bugs!

Live spiders, millipedes and centipedes aren't insects because they have more than six legs. In fact, they may have hundreds of tiny jointed legs! "Millipede" means 1,000 legs, but none of the 8,000 kinds of millipedes actually has that many. Some just have a few dozen. "Centipede" means 100 legs, but the 3,000 types of centipedes have anywhere from just 40 to about 340 legs. Both groups like to live in damp, dark places.

## How do we tell centipedes and millipedes apart?

It's easy! No matter how many legs either 'pede has, millipedes always have two pairs of legs on each body segment, while centipedes always have one pair per body segment. They both walk by moving their many legs in a coordinated wavelike fashion.

## Are they different in any other ways?

Millipedes are shaped like long cylinders, and they have short antennae. They look like a cross between a caterpillar and an earthworm. Centipedes, on the other hand, are flat. They have long antennae to feel for their prey, large pincerlike jaws, and they move very quickly!

I've never seen a bug with so many legs!

**Largest centipede:** The giant centipede of the Central American tropics can be 12 inches long.

**Largest millipede:** The African giant black millipede can grow to 11 inches long and is as thick as a human thumb.

**Most legs, centipede:** 346

**Most legs, millipede:** 400

**How long do centipedes live?** Up to six years

How many pairs of legs do you count on each body segment of this centipede?

*Millipedes can curl up into protective balls.*

## Are millipedes good parents?

Most millipedes just drop their eggs on the ground and leave. However, others spin a cocoon of silk around the egg mass or hide the eggs in an underground chamber. Mothers in a few millipede species even stay in the underground nest with the eggs and guard their young after they've hatched.

## Are centipedes and millipedes dangerous?

The small centipedes in North America are only about an inch long, but they are quick predators that can run down their insect and earthworm prey and stun them with a pinch from their poison claws. Some of the larger tropical centipedes, up to a foot long, have been known to cause painful bites to humans. Millipedes, however, would rather curl up in a ball than bite you! They eat plants because they move too slowly to be predators, although if you bother them, some can release a smelly chemical.

### How do I know how many legs are on a millipede?

It's easy! If you find a millipede, count the body segments, multiply by four, then subtract ten. Got that? Be sure to look closely—some millipedes might have a few legs missing, so the number you end up with may not be quite right.

*How many pairs of legs do you count on each body segment of this millipede?*

# Ancient insects

By now, you have learned about moths that can be the size of plates, beetles as large as your fist, and tiny flying creatures no larger than dots on a page! There also are very, very old insects that have been found in ancient stone fossils and amber. Fossils are formed when a creature settles into fine dirt sediment, and that sediment is buried and compressed over time by the soil and rock.

And to think, I was starting to feel ancient!

Damselflies rest with their wings folded over their backs.

These are no fly-by-night bugs! They've been around!

## What are the most primitive insects?

Dragonflies, damselflies, mayflies, and stoneflies are some of the best-known primitive insects. They all begin life as water-dwelling nymphs. Giant dragonflies have been found in fossils dating to more than 300 million years ago! That means those critters were flying around when dinosaurs roamed the Earth! Other primitive insects include springtails and lice.

## What is the difference between dragonflies and damselflies?

Damselflies are close relatives of dragonflies, but are smaller and much thinner. Damselflies have eyes set far apart on their heads and wings that fold back when they're resting. The eyes of dragonflies, in contrast, are set closer together, and their wings stretch out to their sides when they rest. Dragonfly and damselfly adults are both skilled fliers, and they eat other insects that they catch while flying. The nymphs of both insects are prehistoric-looking carnivores.

**Oldest insect stone fossil found:** A 400 million year old fossil of a springtail

**Oldest amber with insect inside:** 130 million years old. An ant was found in an 80–million–year–old fossil from New Jersey, United States

**Number of dragonflies and damselflies:** 5,000 kinds

**Number of mayflies:** 2,000 kinds

**Number of stoneflies:** More than 1,500 kinds

**Number of compartments in a dragonfly's compound eye:** About 25,000

▲ Mayfly nymphs are distinguished by their three "tails" and the breathing structures on their backs.

## What is the difference between stoneflies and mayflies?

Stonefly nymphs as well as mayfly nymphs live in the water and spend one to three years underwater before developing into winged adults. Stonefly nymphs eat small plants and animals, while mayfly nymphs eat small plants and algae. All mayfly adults, and most kinds of stoneflies, have no digestive system. This means that the adults cannot eat— they only exist to mate. Adult mayflies appear in summer and are identified by their long, thin tails and habit of flying in dense swarms near water and around lights close to the water. They mate and die within hours.

▼ Stonefly nymphs have two "tails," and are found in stony rivers in Britain.

## Do stonefly nymphs make their own shelter?

Yes. That's how they got their name! Female stoneflies deposit their eggs in water, where fish and other creatures can eat the soft-bodied nymphs. So, when they hatch, the vulnerable nymphs use stones to make protective homes.

## Where do lice live?

There are two basic kinds of lice. Book lice live in books and eat molds that grow on the paper. These tiny creatures might be seen scurrying across pages of an old book—they're only about one-tenth of an inch long. Other lice live in animals' hair or feathers and suck blood. They're hard to remove because their front claws can grip so strongly. Head lice cannot fly; instead, they're spread by close contact with other people who have head lice. We can get rid of them by using special shampoos.

▼ Lice that live on people grip hair with their tiny claws.

# All About Camouflage

I'm the only stick with eyes!

Have you ever admired a plant in your backyard when suddenly you realized that one of its leaves was moving? Or, maybe you've noticed something small—jumping across the lawn—but you can't seem to see it when it has stopped hopping and is hiding in the grass.

Many insects sport certain colors that help them blend in with their environments. This helps keep them safe from predators, who can't easily spot them when they are, for example, standing on a tree limb, crouching among blades of grass, or sipping nectar from a flower. Other insects use camouflage to their advantage, waiting for an unsuspecting meal to wander by. Insects aren't the only ones to make use of camouflage. For example, chameleons are lizards that are famous for being able to change their body colors to match their surroundings!

### BLENDING FOR PROTECTION

Moths, the relatively drab-looking cousins of butterflies, are dull by design. Most moths are nocturnal and rest out in the open during the day, but it's very hard to find them because their coloration allows them to blend right in with tree trunks and vegetation. Sometimes it's more than just color that helps a moth stay hidden. Because of the way moths hold their wings when they rest, the insects often resemble the leaves on which they've landed.

### A PERFECT MATCH

While some are green and hide on green leaves, many other grasshoppers are colored or patterned to resemble the leaf litter on the forest floor. Other grasshoppers live in places where there are no trees, and so they blend in with the pebbles and gravel on the ground.

### KATYDIDS' CAMOUFLAGE

Like the moth, the katydid is nocturnal and also uses its colors to stay safely hidden from predators during the day. Usually bright green, this bug positions itself just right on green leaves, lowering its head and angling its wings. Presto! In the blink of an eye, the katydid seems to have transformed itself into a leaf!

## MASTERS OF DISGUISE

While many insects are colored and shaped like leaves, others closely resemble sticks! More than 600 species of walking sticks —some more than 16 inches long!—manage to go virtually unnoticed! The inchworm, the caterpillar stage of the peppered moth, is another insect that looks like a twig when it stays still.

## HIDE AND SEEK

Like the chameleon, some insects and spiders can even change their colors in order to stay hidden! The crab spider, for example, changes its color to match whatever flower it scuttles across when pursuing its prey.

## A SAFE PLACE TO GROW

Metamorphosis—when a caterpillar turns into a moth or butterfly— is an amazing but extremely vulnerable time in an insect's life cycle. The only protection a butterfly or moth has during this life stage is its chrysalis. The similarity of most chrysalids to shriveled or dead leaves lets butterflies and moths develop safely, hidden in plain sight!

## WINGING IT

When you think of butterflies, you probably think of vibrant colors and glimmering wings, right? Believe it or not, even these typically colorful creatures include species that can easily conceal themselves. For example, the underside of the brilliant blue morpho butterflies' wings are brown, so they can just fold their wings and instantly hide from birds and other predators!

## DID THAT THORN MOVE?

It could have—if it was really an insect called a treehopper. When this very small insect clings to branches, it resembles a thorn. That's a very pointed way to blend in!

# Fish & sea creatures

Have you ever watched fish swim in a pond, creek, or aquarium? Fish are vertebrates. Most have two pairs of fins, which help them move in the water. Fish breathe by passing water through their gills, so that they can remove oxygen from the water. There are about 20,000 species of fish, and they live in many different habitats. Some survive in saltwater or freshwater habitats, while others thrive in the **brackish** water of estuaries. There are fish that even live deep in polar seas that are so cold the fish rely on a chemical in their bloodstream to keep them from freezing!

Clownfish

Giant Pacific octopus

Sea urchins

Scorpion fish

Moray eel

Fish living in different habitats eat different things, including algae and other plants, insects—and even fish or other vertebrates! Each species of fish has a different mouth shape and tooth type, which allow each fish to eat particular types of food. You can look at a fish's mouth and tell what it eats. For example, the pike, a fish that preys on other fish, reptiles, and even small birds and mammals, has a long mouth full of sharp teeth that is well-suited for eating these types of creatures. Suckers and carp are bottom-feeders. Because they munch on dead animal and plant matter on the bottom of streams and ponds, they have mouths that are turned downward. One fish, the archerfish, has even developed the ability to "spit" at insects sitting on plants floating on the water's surface. This knocks the insects into the water—then the fish swallows them up!

Most fish also lay eggs. Some fish lay eggs in the water, others make nests, and still others give birth to live young! Carp and their goldfish cousins, for instance, lay their eggs in warm, shallow water, where the eggs can rest on underwater plants. Goldfish lay up to 500 eggs over the course of several days; large female carp can lay up to two million eggs! Sunfish and bass make nests. They swish their tails on the water's bottom to clear out a circular area, where the female lays her eggs. The sun then warms the eggs in the shallow water. (As you might imagine, it's hard for fish to sit on their eggs!) The young of seahorses develop in yet another way. A female seahorse places her eggs in her mate's belly pouch where he then incubates the eggs and protects the young once they emerge.

Fish are some of the most fascinating and unusual creatures on Earth. Fish thrive in tiny freshwater ponds and streams, yet they can also be found almost five miles below the surface of the ocean where there is absolutely no light! Who knows what sea creatures are yet to be discovered?

*Coral reef* ▶

# Reef fish

Let's explore my home!

The most colorful of all fish are the reef fish, which live in the clear waters around ocean reefs. Reef fish, like most fish with colors in their scales, can see in color. Food around these reefs is so abundant that fish in these waters are very plentiful—and in such crowded conditions, color vision comes in handy. It allows these fish to distinguish their own kind from all other fish.

## Is one group of reef fish more colorful than others?

A particular group of reef fish, called the "butterflyfish" group, was named for the diversity of coloration in its family. Their colors reminded scientists of the brilliance of butterflies. Each species in this colorful family carries its own beautiful pattern of spots, stripes, zigzags, and dots, which helps the fish recognize their own kind among the many colorful reef fish. Life can be dangerous, however, for colorful fish because they are so visible in the environment. So, these small fish hover around the hard branches of coral and can dart back inside for protection within seconds.

Butterflyfish confuse predators with their spots and stripes.

## How do reef fish protect themselves from predators?

Clownfish hide in sea anemones for protection.

Some fish, such as clownfish, live in anemones where their predators would be harmed by the anemone's stings. Other fish, like slow-moving boxfish and porcupinefish, have spines on the outside of their bodies for protection. Lionfish have fan-shaped fins, some tipped with sharp spines that can inject poison into their predators! The dark stripes of the lionfish give a clear warning sign to predators to stay away.

My friend Nemo and his dad live in an anemone.

**Largest reef fish:** Giant grouper, over 8 feet long and 650 pounds

**Largest reef:** Great Barrier Reef, Australia; 1,250 miles long, largest object ever built by living things!

**Number of corals:** 800–1,000 species

## Do reef fish all live on the protected side of reefs?

Surprisingly, no. The forcepsfish and a few other reef fish actually live on the side of the reef where breaking waves roll in from the open ocean. In this harsh environment, the small forcepsfish uses its tweezerlike mouth to pick up small animals from nooks and crannies in the reef edge.

## Do any reef fish eat the hard coral of the reef?

Coral is formed by colonies of soft animals that make hard cases to protect themselves. Parrotfish have developed special mouthparts used for eating the coral—their hard beaks can break it off. They even grind the food up twice—once in their mouth and again in their throat, where the parrotfish have another set of grinding teeth!

## Why do some fish have noticeable spots near their tails?

The spots on a fish's tail, which might look like eyes to another animal, help to confuse predators. Fish normally can escape from a predator by quickly swimming forward. If a predator thinks the fish is headed in the opposite direction, the misdirected predator will miss its meal!

▼ *Many differently colored fish live in coral-reef habitats.*

# Salmon & trout

Salmon are some of the most interesting kinds of fish. Did you know that they are famous for migrating up cold freshwater streams? Adults migrate upstream to **spawn**. The babies that hatch swim down to a lake or the ocean to eat plankton. As they grow larger, they eat other fish. Years later, they migrate back up the same streams where their own parents made their successful nests of eggs.

Keep swimming! Keep swimming!

## Where do trout live?

Trout thrive in clean, cold-water streams and lakes with healthy insect populations. Trout eat the larvae and adults of mayflies, mosquitoes, black flies, and other insects that live around these flowing streams.

## How do salmon grow?

A baby salmon that has hatched from its egg and become active is called a "fry." It feeds on small crustaceans or other organisms, and grows, and develops blotches, or "parr marks," on its side. At this stage, it's called a "parr." When it is two to six years old, the parr marks disappear and the newly silver "smolt" swims out to sea to become an adult salmon.

◀ *Adult salmon migrate upstream to spawn.*

**Largest brown trout:** Over 40 pounds

**Largest salmon:** King salmon; over 5 feet long, and about 100 pounds

**Number of eggs:** Atlantic salmon; more than 21,000 at one time

**Number of salmon and trout species:** More than 300

There are more than 300 kinds of salmon and trout.

## How do salmon find their home streams?

Because of the unique plants, minerals, and insects living in each stream, salmon can remember the taste and memorize the odor of the stream where it hatched, and **migrate** to it from large lakes, or even from the ocean, many miles away. Chinook salmon return home from up to 2,000 miles away to lay their eggs! We know that salmon use their sense of smell to find their way home because researchers interested in how salmon migrate once blocked some salmons' nostrils. They found that the fish not permitted to smell could not find their way.

## Do salmon eat when they swim upstream to spawn?

In an exceptional show of endurance, salmon swim upstream, often for hundreds of miles, without feeding. When they finish spawning, they are thin and exhausted. Many die or are eaten by predators such as bears during the spawning run.

You can tell "parr" stage salmon by their blotches.

### Where can I go to see fish outside an aquarium?

You can sometimes watch salmon swimming up "fish ladders" during the fall breeding season, or see them being fed at hatcheries. Talk to your parents or a state fish biologist about fish-watching opportunities in your area!

# Fast predators of the sea

Did you know that water is eight hundred times denser than air? It is hard to move quickly through water unless you are sharply pointed at the front, with a strong tail at the back and smooth scales with a slippery covering to help you speed through the water. The predators of the world's seas and lakes have all of these features. Many of the fastest fish, such as tuna and sailfish, are shaped just like torpedoes!

*If you're talking about fast, dude, you have to ride the Eastern Australian current!*

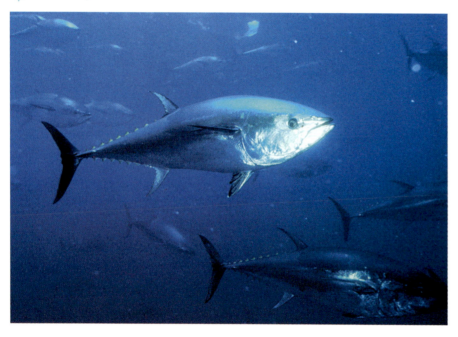

▼ *Tuna are fast predators.*

## Are mackerels fast swimmers?

Although mackerels can weigh up to 100 pounds, they are speedy fish that swim in the ocean in schools. When these high-speed predators attack prey, they travel in packs, similar to the way wolves do. The prey fish hunted by mackerels often swim closely together for protection, forming tight groups that can confuse the mackerels.

## What is a tuna fish?

Tuna are predatory fish that swim in schools, but move in irregular patterns while searching for prey. Although scientists have found that schools of tuna move between three and a half miles per hour and eight miles per hour, individual tuna fish have been clocked at speeds above 50 miles per hour!

Different kinds of tuna live in different habitats. The northern bluefin is the largest tuna species—the largest one ever caught weighed over 1,400 pounds! Bluefins, which live in shallow water over the flat sea bottoms that extend out from shore, also migrate long distances in the oceans. Yellowfin and skipjack tuna, meanwhile, often stay near reef walls that drop from the shallow reef down into the deep sea.

**Speed record, sailfish:** Swim almost 70 miles per hour

**Speed record, swordfish:** Swim more than 50 miles per hour

**Speed record, mackerel:** Almost 20 miles per hour

**Tarpon size:** Over 8 feet long, weigh over 350 pounds; Female tarpon may produce 12 million eggs!

**Tarpon predators:** Sharks, dolphins, and alligators

**Maximum depth of swim, tarpon:** 100 feet

## What is a tarpon?

Tarpon are extraordinary fish. They usually live in the Atlantic Ocean near shore, but can tolerate the absence of salt in freshwater rivers. As adults, large tarpon can move quickly from ocean to freshwater habitat and back. But what's even more amazing is that they have a special air-filled pouch called a "**swim bladder**" that is different from the swim bladders in other fish. When tarpons swim into water that doesn't have enough oxygen for them to absorb through their gills, they gulp air into this pouch to get the oxygen they need!

▼ *Tarpon eat fish and large crustaceans.*

▼ *A school of jack mackerel*

## Why it's good to be in a school

If you were a fish, would you swim alone or in a school?

Some scientists who study animal behavior (**ethologists**) think that fish travel in schools because there is safety in numbers—when predators come around, fish in a school have a better chance of remaining unnoticed (and uneaten!). The more predators lurking in an area, the safer it will be for the fish to live in a big school.

It also helps to be near animals that eat the same food you eat—the sooner they can find food, the sooner you can eat, too! In schools that include different sizes of fish, the big fish eat first. Ethologists have found that, within a school, small fish like to travel with other small fish to reduce the competition for food.

Fish form schools when they are moving. It is easier to swim in the back of the school, but fish in front tend to find and eat more food than those at the back.

# Sharks, skates & rays

Did you know that sharks, skates, and rays are not really fish? They belong to a different class of animals than true fish. Unlike the gills of true fish, sharks' gills aren't covered, and so their gill slits are visible. Their bodies are covered with small scales called "denticles." Sharks' most recognizable features are their rows of large teeth and the **dorsal** fin on the top of their body.

> My name is Bruce, and I'm a nice fish.

## What is the largest shark?

The whale shark is the largest of all living sharks and fish. It is not really a whale, because whales are mammals. But it is the size of a whale—it can grow to be 50 feet long and weigh about 20 tons (40,000 pounds)! The basking shark is another one of the largest creatures in the world's oceans. Unfortunately, we know very little about them, except that they are huge plankton feeders.

▼ The whale shark is the world's largest shark.

Hammerhead sharks sometimes eat rays.

**Largest ray:** Manta ray, also called devil ray; about 20 feet across

**Smallest shark:** Dwarf shark; 10 inches long

**Fastest shark:** Mako, found in warm waters worldwide; up to 55 miles per hour!

**Fun fact:** A shark egg case is called a "mermaid's purse."

Each shark loses about 25,000 teeth in a lifetime!

## Are great white sharks truly dangerous?

All sharks are expert predators, but most sharks do not hunt people—even great whites. To sharks, people paddling on surf-boards may look like seals from underneath. Since great whites hunt seals, they could mistake a person for prey.

## Do sharks eat other sharks?

Yes. Hammerhead sharks, for example, have been found with stingray tail-fin spines stuck in their mouths. And nurse sharks have been known to eat smaller sharks. There are more than 500 different kinds of sharks and rays, each of which specializes in eating foods that can range in size from small crabs and shellfish to marine mammals larger than humans!

I have to keep reminding myself: fish are friends, not food!

## What are rays and skates?

Rays and skates, flattened sea creatures with long tails, are closely related to sharks. Most skates and rays eat bottom-dwelling creatures, but some hunt actively swimming fish.

Manta rays can grow to be more than 25 feet wide.

# Bottom-dwelling fish

Bottom-dwelling fish are well adapted to their environment. They often have flat bottoms to help them move around more easily, and their mouth is on the underside of their head. They eat crustaceans, insects, plants, and other small organisms in their environment. Bottom dwellers include suckers in streams, carp in ponds, sturgeon in rivers and lakes, and flatfish in oceans.

My friend Nemo has been everywhere—he's seen fish from the bottom on up!

The armored catfish is a bottom-dwelling fish.

## What kinds of fish live on the bottom of ponds and small lakes?

Common carp, goldfish, and their relatives live in warm-water ponds and lakes with thick, weedy bottoms. Carp and goldfish are both minnows. All minnows chew their food with teeth that are in their throats, behind their gill areas—these teeth are called pharyngeal teeth. Young carp eat bottom-living crustaceans and insect larvae, while older carp eat vegetation.

## Which bottom-dwelling fish live in rivers and large lakes?

Sturgeons live in these kinds of habitats. Sturgeons look rather sharklike; they have a similarly shaped tail and a downward-facing mouth, out of which they can thrust a tubelike structure that vacuums up food as they cruise along the bottom. Have you ever tasted caviar? Sturgeons are known to produce millions of eggs that can be served as caviar, which many people consider a delicacy.

## How do suckers eat?

Suckers, which live in North America and Asia, get their name from their downward-facing mouths and thick, suckerlike lips. Have you ever slurped juice from a glass? That's similar to the way suckers eat; they swim along the bottom of the stream using their special mouths to slurp up debris and small organisms. Clearly, they don't have the best manners!

**Longest-lived carp:** Over 40 years

**Largest sucker:** White sucker, North America; over 2 feet long

**Largest sturgeon:** Beluga sturgeon, Russia; 15 feet long, 3,000 pounds

**Largest flatfish:** Pacific halibut; over 8 feet long, over 800 pounds

Sturgeon are among the most primitive fish in the world.

Some of my best friends are bottom dwellers.

### Do flatfish start their lives in the ocean looking like their parents?

No. Flatfish go through a metamorphosis. Newly hatched sole, flounder, and other flatfish float around above the bottom of the ocean, looking a lot like tiny fish. But soon enough, one eye starts to migrate toward the other eye! Then, the fish's mouth changes shape. The eyes end up on the side of the fish that faces up and is camouflaged to match the ocean bottom, while the underside of the fish stays white. Pretty cool, right? The flatfish then starts living life as a true bottom dweller.

This flounder has changed color to blend in with its surroundings.

# Poisonous & venomous fish

Over the centuries, humans have been known to get sick—or even die—from getting stung by, or eating, venomous or poisonous fish. Most of these incidents happen by accident, when people have come into contact with these creatures by mistake. Believe it or not, these fish may even be useful—an ancient Roman author and scientist named Pliny actually used ground stingray stingers to relieve toothaches!

I'm not fat, I'm puffy!

Sea urchins have venomous spines.

## How many poisonous and venomous fish are there in the world?

Lots! Scientists estimate there are about 500 different kinds of poisonous and venomous fish in the world. They are especially numerous around small islands and reefs in the Pacific.

## What are some of the most venomous fish?

Actually, some of the most venomous creatures in the sea aren't fish, but rather different kinds of shells, starfish, or jellies. Sea wasps, a kind of jellyfish, have a deadly sting. Other venomous ocean dwellers include octopuses, cone shells, sea urchins, sea cucumbers, and the crown-of-thorns starfish.

The Australian blue-ringed octopus can kill with one bite!

**Poisonous shark:** Greenland shark; flesh is poisonous to people

**Man-killer:** Stonefish; great camouflage, venom powerful enough to kill humans!

**Armor plus:** Boxfish; A repellant poison oozes over its bony plates.

**Venomous octopus:** Blue-ringed octopus, Australia; Painless bite can kill a human in an hour—when the poison takes effect!

Bearded scorpionfish can be found in the Caribbean.

That fish over there is venomous! At least I think it is.

## How do venomous fish inject their poison?

Despite their small size, creatures such as the scorpionfish can give you a nasty little sting with the spines found on their backs and heads. When the venomous spine on the scorpionfish cuts the victim's skin, venom is pumped in from a gland in the fish. Scorpionfish, which belong to the same family as lionfish and stonefish, are a hazard to divers, since these fish are often camouflaged to blend in with their background.

## Is there a way to tell venomous fish from other fish?

Some venomous fish have bright colors, while others have large spines that we can spot instantly. But beware, these are just general rules—many venomous fish can be identified only by experts!

Pufferfish inflate their stomachs with water or air when in danger.

## Puffers

Pufferfish are very poisonous. They gulp down water to make themselves "puff up"—this helps to scare away enemies. About 100 kinds of pufferfish are found in the tropical and subtropical waters of the Atlantic, Pacific, and Indian Oceans, including some found around coral reefs. Strangely enough, the Japanese have developed a painkiller using puffer poison! And, even though the poison of this fish can be deadly, the pufferfish is considered a tasty meal in Japan.

# Eels

I'm glad there aren't any eels in the fish tank with us. They eat fish!

Long ago, people believed that these weird-looking creatures grew out of horse hairs that were blown into the water! Now we know that common eels lay their eggs in the Sargasso Sea in the Atlantic Ocean. Their babies grow up, then make the long swim to freshwater rivers in North America. In these rivers, the adults may spend their winters buried in river mud or beneath underwater rocks, and then reappear in warm weather.

## What kinds of eels are there?

The several hundred different kinds of eels include common eels in freshwater rivers, as well as conger eels, pike eels, snake eels, and moray eels in the oceans. Most eels have smooth outer skin, and they move by weaving from side to side, like snakes. They have a top, or dorsal, fin that looks almost like a ribbon and runs along their bodies.

I knew the ocean was dangerous! There are eels in there!

▲ Seychelles moray eels are found in the Indian and Pacific Oceans.

## Why are eels so long and narrow?

The eel's long shape might seem strange, but it's actually quite useful. It helps the eel squeeze into small crevices and other tight places where it can find prey. Moray eels squeeze their colorful bodies into their lairs and then attack the fish swimming past. Conger eels hide with only their heads sticking out from their crevices during the day. At night, they emerge to hunt slow-moving crabs, lobsters, and other ocean creatures.

**Number of species of eels:** Several hundred, in about 20 major groups or "families"

**Longest freshwater eel:** 5 feet long

**Longest conger eel:** 9 feet long

**Longest moray eel:** 10 feet long

**Greatest depth gulper eel (an eel-like fish) found:** 1,530 fathoms = 9,180 feet

## How many eggs do eels lay?

A whole lot! Eels participate in an incredible migration that is in the reverse direction of salmon migration. Common eels hatch from millions of eggs in the ocean, then migrate to freshwater, and end their lives as adults in the Sargasso Sea where they were born. Each common eel female lays more than 100,000 eggs at the end of this migration. Their babies look like tiny leaves and are transparent during their first year, making them almost invisible to predators in the ocean.

▲ Baby eels are called "elvers."

## How long can eels live?

Longer than you may think! Male common eels live in fresh water for six to twelve years and females for nine to twenty years before returning to the ocean to spawn. During their lives, common eels travel thousands of miles, but once they return to their spawning area, they die. Captive eels do not need to migrate to spawn, and so they live longer in captivity than in the wild. One captive common eel lived for 85 years in captivity!

◀ Moray eels are nocturnal.

Hey dude, the oldest eel is a baby compared to me!

# Crabs, octopuses & shellfish

There are many marine animals living in the sea which are not considered to be true fish, such as crabs, octopuses, and shellfish. One type of shellfish, the abalone, produces glittering "mother-of-pearl" that is used to make jewelry. Others, like queen conchs, mussels, and scallops have beautiful shell shapes and textures. All of these creatures depend on clean oceans to survive.

Dad, if clownfish aren't always funny, does that mean that crabs aren't always crabby?

## What is a horseshoe crab?

Horseshoe crabs, once called "horsefoot crabs" because their shells look like a horse's foot, aren't crabs at all—they are related to scorpions, spiders, and ticks! Horseshoe crabs look dangerous because of their long, sharp tails, but they just use this nonvenomous spine to plow through sand on the ocean bottom and roll over when they are accidentally flipped onto their backs. Horseshoe crabs, which aren't full-grown adults until they are nine to twelve years old, mate only a few days each spring and early summer, when the tides are suitable. Females, which are larger than the males, crawl to the high-tide line, passing through large groups of males, to lay their eggs in the sand of their favorite nesting beaches.

Horseshoe crabs form large groups during mating season.

**Largest arthropod:** Japanese spider crab, Pacific Ocean; legs 12 feet across; The Japanese spider crab is the world's largest crustacean and largest crab.

**Largest Octopus:** Giant Pacific octopus, record 600 pounds

**Largest Clam:** Giant clam; 3 feet across, 650 pounds

△ Fiddler crabs have eyes on stalks so they can look in two directions at once!

## What is a fiddler crab?

Fiddler crabs are one of the most visible inhabitants of the ocean's intertidal zone. They love salt marsh habitats where they can create burrows in the mudbanks, and they can often be seen along the banks of salt marsh streams when the tide is out. There are several different kinds of fiddlers, all preferring different habitats.

## How did the fiddler crab gets its name?

Fiddler crabs do a sort of "fiddle" and "dance." Male fiddler crabs, which have one claw that is much larger than the other, wave that claw back and forth in the air to attract females. At the same time, they stomp their legs! They also wave this large claw to show their rivals that the area is under their control.

## Is it true that the octopus is one of the smartest invertebrates?

Absolutely! Octopuses are probably the smartest invertebrates of all. They have a very good memory, and they can even be trained to tell the difference between various shapes and patterns. Giant octopuses in aquariums have also learned how to unscrew caps from jars just by watching a person do it, and they can perform other complex tasks. Most octopuses live only about three or four years.

▽ Giant Pacific octopuses are very smart for invertebrates.

My dad is the smartest octopus I know.

# Unusual water dwellers

There are many unusual animals living in waters all over the world. They can be shaped like stars, resemble tiny horses, or just look like shapeless blobs! Some have fins and tails, while others have tentacles. They can be less than an inch long or as big as 300 pounds and the size of a washing machine! However, many of these creatures—including paddlefish, jellyfish, or starfish—are not true fish.

I'm $H_2O$ intolerant. Ah–choo!

Eggs fill the belly pouch of this male seahorse.

## What are plankton?

Plankton are animals or plants that cannot swim, or swim very weakly, that are moved around in the water by currents and tides. Plankton include tiny animals such as crustaceans, and even plants like algae, which float on the surface of the ocean. Plankton are not always small—the biggest plankton are animals we call jellyfish. Jellyfish move so weakly that currents carry them through the ocean. One of the largest of all jellies is the Portuguese man-of-war, which has a large "swimming bell" that helps the organism float through tropical ocean waters. The man-of-war, also called a "sea nettle," has deadly tentacles that are more than eight feet long and dangle from its bell. These filaments contain stinging cells that kill animals such as fish, which are the prey of this jelly.

## Is a seahorse a fish?

Seahorses are unusual fish with stiff body armor, and grasping (prehensile) tails that can be used like hooks to hang on to coral or weeds. Seahorses hold themselves upright with the help of small whirring **pectoral fins** and their dorsal fins, which act like small engines that move the sea horse forward. Seahorses feed on tiny animals they suck up into their tubelike mouths.

**Anglerfish:** Unusual true fish with "fishing lure" spine above mouth

**Catfish:** Fleshy barbels by mouth look like cat's whiskers; 2,500 species worldwide

**Dogfish:** Small, mostly bottom-dwelling shark; 60 species worldwide

**Cuttlefish:** A flattened relative of octopus and squid

**Sea mouse:** Segmented worm with green "fur;" burrows along seabed

# Are there different kinds of jellies?

There are two kinds of jellies—Siphonophores and Scypozoans. Siphonophore jellies may look like they are one large animal, but they are really a group of small animals working together. Scypozoans are true jellyfish. They are a single, large animal. The giant jellyfish is the biggest of the true jellies—one of these organisms, found more than 100 years ago, had a floating bell over seven feet in diameter and tentacles over 120 feet long—stretched out, this creature would have been more than 245 feet across! That would make the giant jellyfish the world's longest animal!

▼ *Sea nettles like this are often found near shore.*

▲ *Paddlefish open their mouths wide to feed on plankton.*

# What are paddlefish?

Paddlefish are strange-looking relatives of the sturgeon. Only two species of paddlefish are known—one native to the Mississippi River in North America, and one from the Yangtze River in China. These fish hatch with just a small bump on the end of their snout, but eventually their paddlelike snout grows to one-third the length of their bodies. Paddlefish swim around with their mouths wide open, eating small plankton floating in the river.

# Strange but True Fish Tales

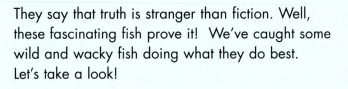

They say that truth is stranger than fiction. Well, these fascinating fish prove it! We've caught some wild and wacky fish doing what they do best. Let's take a look!

These fish rock, dude!

▲ Anglerfish

## LIGHTING UP THE OCEAN

It's so dark in the deepest parts of the ocean that some fish need to produce their own light—so they glow in the dark! Different bioluminescent fish—fish that generate light—glow for different reasons. Some are avoiding predators, some are looking to attract prey, and others are trying to charm a potential mate. The hatchetfish uses light as camouflage; by blending in with the dark water below and natural light above, it hides from predators. The shining tubeshoulder releases a glowing slime to distract predators and escape. The anglerfish uses the glowing, rodlike spine on its forehead as a lure to attract prey. Lanternfish looking for mates produce light from organs along their sides and belly. Each species has a different, distinct pattern of lights. Lanternfish find their mates by looking for another fish that produces the same light pattern. Now that's love at first sight—or light!

## THOSE FISH ARE REALLY OLD!

The coelacanth is an ocean fish thought to have gone extinct over 65 million years ago, around the same time as the dinosaurs. Amazingly, this ancient fish species was rediscovered in 1938, swimming in the Indian Ocean!

Coelacanthe ▶

## GETTING ALONG — SWIMMINGLY!

A number of coral reef fish, including the black grouper, routinely become infested with parasites. When that happens, these fish pay a visit to the cleaners—smaller fish that remove the parasites as well as dead skin. Why don't the larger fish just eat the fish that clean them off? No one really knows for sure, but it looks like the larger fish feel so much better after their parasites are removed that they leave the cleaning fish alone. Cleaning fish, which include wrasses and gobies, get free food by eating the parasites and don't have to worry about predators. In fact, some fish have even been seen lining up to wait their turn to be groomed by a coral reef fish!

▲ *Wrasse*

## WHAT A MOUTHFUL!

Some fish parents carry their eggs in their mouths until they hatch! The banded yellow mouthbrooder, for instance, lays her eggs in the water. Once they've been fertilized, she scoops them up in her mouth and keeps it closed until the eggs hatch. For several weeks, she doesn't even open her mouth to eat! Even after the eggs hatch, the babies stay safe inside her mouth a little while longer. Only after they swim off does the very hungry mother finally go find food. In other fish, such as jawfish and arawanas, the male is the one who holds the eggs in his mouth.

*These baby fish are called alevins.* ▶

## A BREATH OF FRESH AIR?

Although all fish have gills, some also have lungs. In fact, there are fish called lungfish, which are found in muddy freshwater swamps in Australia, Africa, and South America, where there's sometimes not enough oxygen in the water. While the lungfish usually breathes with its gills, it sometimes comes up to the surface when it needs more oxygen and takes in a big gulp of air.

Did you know that archerfish are known to shoot water out of their mouths to knock spiders and other insects from low-hanging leaves? The tambaqui sometimes leaps out of its Amazon River home to snag food from trees lining the riverbanks. And the arawana, another South American fish, which catches and even eats small birds and bats, can leap six feet out of the water for its food!

◀ *Arawana*

# Helping animals thrive

By now, you've discovered some of the largest, smallest, fastest, slowest, and most unusual creatures in the animal world! Many people choose careers in which they research animals, work to protect animals through conservation organizations, or care for animals individually. Here are a few of the people who spend their lives helping animals:

**Veterinarians**, or animal doctors, work to keep animals' bodies healthy. They examine animals to see if they are in good health, and make sure their diet and excercise levels meet their needs. Vets also care for and cure sick animals.

**Zookeepers** feed and tend to animals living in zoos. They also enhance the lives of these animals with ever-changing foods, training, and toys. They also try to make each animal's zoo habitat similar to its natural one. This is called "animal enrichment." Many zoos worldwide use animal enrichment to keep their animals happy, healthy, and mentally stimulated. Another important part of a zookeeper's job is to train the animals to accept health exams done by zoo veterinarians. Sometimes, they train animals to be calm while giving blood in case veterinarians need to test the animal's blood for signs of illness.

**Animal nutritionists** work with animals in the wild to discover what kinds of food each animal needs. Then they develop healthy food mixes for animals that live in zoos and that are cared for by humans.

**Animal behavior scientists, wildlife biologists, and ecologists** help us understand why animals behave the way they do. They study animals in the wild and in zoos and research centers, and teach us about what animals need to survive. Their work helps people better manage animals' habitats, and populations in the wild, while keeping zoo animals healthy, too. This knowlege will help to keep our planet healthy for future generations.

# True conservation heroes

Now that you've learned about how people help animals, meet some true heroes of conservation, people who work in zoos and wildlife parks dedicated to the preservation of animals. Their work today will continue to be important to the wellbeing and survival of many species for generations to come. Many people throughout the world are working hard to save different species; these are just a few of them. With so many animals in trouble on our planet today, we need more heroes. Will you be one someday?

## Zoo Biologists Make a Difference

More than 20 years ago, Dr. **Bill Conway** of the Bronx Zoo in the United States, and **Luis Jacome** of the Buenos Aires Zoo and fundacion BioAndina in Argentina, dreamed of saving condors in the wild. The huge condor, with its red-skinned, bald head and reputation for killing sheep and other domestic animals, was a bird not many people cared about saving. But the condor's habitat was changing—and so condors were disappearing.

At that time, the Bronx Zoo and other zoos were working to breed rescued, injured, and rehabilitated California and Andean condors in captivity. Zookeepers raised condor chicks using condor-head-shaped hand puppets, so the young birds would grow up without becoming too accustomed to people and could be returned to the wild.

Luis decided to reintroduce the zoo-raised condors to the Patagonia region of Argentina. He spent months getting to know local Patagonian farmers and ranchers, and helped start environmental education programs to teach people to respect the large birds.

When the first condors raised in captivity were about to be released, Luis held a ceremony to help build support for the birds.

The ceremony's attendees watched as the condors were released to the wild. To keep track of how many would survive, the scientists attached solar-powered satellite transmitters to the condors. This allowed them to study the birds' flight patterns, habitat preferences, roost site locations, and other behaviors to monitor their survival.

Thanks to Luis Jacome and Bill Conway, condors have been returned to the wild to once again soar majestically through the South American skies.

## Commited People Make a Difference

As a child, **Dr. Ullas Karanth** was deeply interested in wildlife. He was especially interested in tigers, which have cultural importance in India.

When Ullas went to college, he read an article about the first-ever scientific study of tigers in India. Unsustainable forestry practices throughout India and Myanmar had decreased the tiger's forest habitat. The great cats could only live in "reserved forests," areas protected from clearing and farming. Ullas decided to join the international effort for tiger conservation and become a wildlife biologist.

As Dr. Karanth began to study tigers in the wild, he began to suspect that officials were overestimating tiger numbers. He designed a way to estimate numbers reliably, then walked through trails with forest rangers counting hoofed animals and collecting tiger droppings for later analysis. Dr. Karanth also put radio collars on some tigers and would spend his days on foot or on the back of an elephant with his receiver tracking these tigers.

Dr. Karanth and his colleagues found out many things about tigers. Each tiger needs more than 5,000 pounds of food per year, which means each tiger needs to kill and eat more than 50 prey animals annually. If tigers do not have a large enough habitat, or if local poachers compete with them by taking too many prey, the tigers can barely eke out an existence.

Today, Dr. Karanth works with local communities to encourage their interest in saving tigers. He uses his scientific studies of tiger biology to inform conservationists. He also talks with everyone from the highest government officials to the villagers in tiger country about how to preserve the tiger's survival as a species. Dr. Karanth, a leader in tiger conservation, is committed to helping prevent the extinction of this incredible, awesome, and powerful big cat.

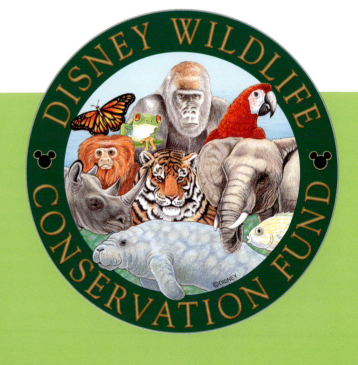

## A Student Lab Worker Becomes Ecologist and Conservationist

In college, **Anne Savage** worked in her university's laboratory taking care of small South American monkeys called cotton-top tamarins. As a result, she decided to focus her studies on monkeys, a science called primatology, and eventually began to study cotton-top tamarins in zoos and in the South American wild. Anne is now director of Proyecto Tití (Spanish for "Project Tamarin"), a conservation program that combines field research, education programs, and community programs to make the conservation of natural resources a priority in Colombia.

Destruction of Columbia's forests may be causing many of its species to become rare or even extinct. With the help of local biologists and communities, Proyecto Tití strives to make the cotton-top tamarins a "flagship species" in its conservation efforts. Flagship species are species that people find easy to care about saving from extinction. Saving these kinds of animals often helps to protect other life forms in the habitat where they live. During the years, Dr. Savage and her colleagues have learned many things about the behavior of cotton-top tamarins. They continue to study critical habitat needs to help them survive into the future.

Proyecto Tití biologists and educators have also established programs to link schoolkids in Colombia and the United States. The kids in these programs learn from one another about the unique animals found in both countries.

### You, too, can make a difference!

As children, these conservation heroes were inspired by the amazing world of animals. It all starts with a simple appreciation and respect for the animals in your world. Who knows where that might take you?

# Many of the animals in this book are helped by the Disney Wildlife Conservation Fund.

The Disney Wildlife Conservation Fund (DWCF) was established in 1995 as a global awards program for the study and protection of the world's wildlife and ecosytems. It provides annual awards to U.S. non-profit conservation organizations working alongside their peers in other countries. Many of the recipient organizations concentrate their activities on "biological hotspots"—areas rich in plant and animal life at risk of imminent destruction. Since its inception, the fund has contributed more than 8.5 million dollars, distributed among 450 projects in more than 30 countries. Each project is evaluated on specific criteria, including scientific methodology, magnitude of need, involvement of partner organizations, ability to impact an area in the near-term, and elements of public education and community involvement.

For fun activities and more information about animals, visit **www.disneywildlifefund.com.**

# Glossary

**Antlers** - Bony growths on the heads of some animals, such as deer. Antlers are shed yearly.

**Bactrians** - Two-humped camels.

**Baleen** - The stiff substance found in the upper jaws of certain whales, which is used to filter food.

**Blubber** - The fatty layer under a whale's skin that helps keep the whale warm.

**Brackish** - A mix of salt and freshwater.

**Calves** - Young whales. The young of some other animals, such as elephants, also are called calves.

**Carapace** - A bony covering on the back of an animal, such as a turtle (See "shell").

**Carnivore** - An animal that eats only meat.

**Carrion** - Dead or decaying flesh.

**Clutch** - A nest of eggs.

**Cold-blooded** - A term for animals that regulate their body temperature using their environment. Reptiles, insects, and fish are cold-blooded.

**Crèche** - A group of young birds, often guarded by one or two adult birds.

**Diurnal** - Active during the day.

**Dorsal fin** - A fin on the top of a fish.

**Dromedaries** - One-humped camels.

**Egg** - The offspring of birds, and many fish, reptiles, insects, and amphibians hatch from eggs.

**Endangered** - In danger of becoming extinct.

**Ethologist** - A scientist who studies animal behavior.

**Facial disk** - The circle of feathers around each eye of an owl.

**Feather follicle** - Small pit on a bird's skin that holds the shaft of each growing feather. During molting, the follicle loosens its grip on the feather's shaft.

**Feather tract** - Part of a bird's skin from which feathers grow. Feathers do not grow on all parts of a bird's body.

**Fluke** - A whale's flattened tail.

**Horns** - Bony growths on the heads of some animals, such as antelope. Horns grow throughout an animal's life.

**Incisor** - Type of tooth adapted for cutting.

**Larva** - A stage in an insect's lifecycle. Larvae are young insects that hatch from eggs.

**Marsupials** - A type of mammal, such as a kangaroo, in which females have a pouch, where the young is protected as it develops.

**Metamorphosis** - The complete transformation that some animals, such as frogs, undergo to develop from young into an adult. When a frog hatches from an egg, it becomes a tadpole (See "tadpole"), and eventually develops into an adult frog.

**Migrate** - To move to a different area or climate from time to time.

**Nocturnal** - Active at night.

**Pectoral fins** - Fins on the sides of a fish. Pectoral fins help fish move around in the water.

**Pigment** - Substance that gives color to birds' feathers.

**Plastron** - The underside of a turtle's shell (See "shell").

**Prehensile** - Adapted for grasping, by wrapping around something. Some monkeys have prehensile tails.

**Preen gland** - A special gland, which produces a waxy oil that birds smooth through their feathers. Preening helps birds remove parasites and bacteria from their feathers.

**Pupa** - A stage in the lifecycle of insects undergoing metamophosis. Larvae grow into pupa before becoming adult insects.

**Quills** - Stiff spines that protect the bodies of some rodents, such as porcupines.

**Resilin** - An elastic protein found in fleas' muscles. Resilin helps fleas jump long distances.

**Rookeries** - A large nesting colony of birds, such as penguins. Some other animals, such as seals, also gather in groups called rookeries to breed.

**Roosting** - The way that birds rest or sleep. Some birds roost alone; others roost in flocks.

**"Round" dance** - One of two types of dances that honeybees do to show fellow bees where to find food. Honeybees perform this dance when food is close to the hive.

**Scavenge** - To feed on carrion (See "carrion").

**Shell** - The hard outer covering on some animals, such as turtles and arthropods.

**Spawn** - To lay eggs. Fish are animals that spawn.

**Swim bladder** - An air-filled sac in many fish that prevents fish from sinking.

**Tadpole** - A young amphibian. Tadpoles look like fish; they have a large "head" and a tail. The "head" will develop into the head and body of the adult frog.

**Talons** - Sharp, hooked claws of some birds. Birds of prey, such as eagles and falcons, use talons to grasp and kill prey.

**Thermals** - Large currents of warm air rising from the ground.

**Tool** - Something a person or animal uses to perform a task more easily.

**Troop** - Group of monkeys.

**Vertebrate** - A type of animal that has a backbone and an internal skeletal system.

**"Waggle" dance** - One of two types of dances that honeybees do to show fellow bees where to find food. Honeybees perform this dance when food is more than 50 yards away from the hive. The direction in which the bee "dances" tells the bees in what direction food can be found.

**Warm-blooded** - A term for animals whose body temperatures stay constant in any environment. Birds and mammals are warm-blooded.

**Whiffling** - The way that some birds land. A bird that descends while tipping from side to side in the air is "whiffling."

# Index

# Photos credits